"How are you doing?" Craig asked.

"What?" Letty replied, startled.

"Your face was almost as red as your hair. I wondered if you were winning the battle or if I should dive for cover."

She scrutinized him with faint uneasiness. "You give me the creepiest feeling; you seem to be able to read my mind."

He chuckled. "It isn't all that difficult. When steam starts to come out of one's ears, the natural assumption is that the person is upset."

"You're going to be a real problem to me."

His blue eyes widened. "Oh? And why is that?"

"You stay so calm. A person with a shotgun mouth like mine always loses an argument to calmness."

"I don't want to argue with you, Letty."

Her head rose slowly, her eyes imprisoned by his gleaming, hypnotic gaze. What *did* he want? She longed but didn't dare to ask.

Dear Reader:

We're celebrating SECOND CHANCE AT LOVE's third birthday with a new cover format! I'm sure you had no trouble recognizing our traditional butterfly logo and distinctive SECOND CHANCE AT LOVE type. But you probably also noticed that the cover artwork is considerably larger than before. We're thrilled with the new look, and we hope you are, too!

In a sense, our new cover treatment reflects what's been happening *inside* SECOND CHANCE AT LOVE books. We're constantly striving to bring you fresh and original romances with unexpected twists and delightful surprises. We introduce promising new writers on a regular basis. And we aim for variety by publishing some romances that are funny, some that are poignant, some that are "traditional," and some that take an entirely new approach. SECOND CHANCE AT LOVE is constantly evolving to meet your need for "something new" in your romance reading.

At the same time, we *haven't* changed the successful editorial concept behind each SECOND CHANCE AT LOVE romance. And we've consistently maintained a reputation for being a line of the highest quality.

So, just like the new covers, SECOND CHANCE AT LOVE romances are satisfyingly familiar—yet excitingly different—and better than ever!

Happy reading,

Ellen Edwards

Ellen Edwards, Senior Editor
SECOND CHANCE AT LOVE
The Berkley Publishing Group
200 Madison Avenue
New York, N.Y. 10016

P.S. Do you receive our SECOND CHANCE AT LOVE and TO HAVE AND TO HOLD newsletter? If not, be sure to fill out the coupon in the back of this book, and we'll send you the newsletter free of charge four times a year.

Second Chance at Love ®

HEAVEN ON EARTH

MARY HASKELL

A
SECOND CHANCE AT LOVE
BOOK

Other books by *Mary Haskell*

Second Chance at Love
SONG FOR A LIFETIME #124
REACH FOR TOMORROW #144
CRAZY IN LOVE #176

To Have and to Hold
HOLD FAST 'TIL DAWN #8
ALL THAT GLITTERS #17

HEAVEN ON EARTH

Requests for permission to make copies of any part of the work should be mailed to: Permissions, Second Chance at Love, The Berkley Publishing Group, 200 Madison Avenue, New York, NY 10016.

First edition published July 1984

First printing

"Second Chance at Love" and the butterfly emblem are trademarks belonging to Jove Publications, Inc.

Printed in the United States of America

Second Chance at Love books are published by
The Berkley Publishing Group
200 Madison Avenue, New York, NY 10016

To my sweet,
fuzzy friend,
Pudge.

- 1 -

LETTY SWUNG INTO the long driveway, noting that the heavy
metal gate had been left open for her. Maneuvering the
wheel with her right hand, she glanced at the watch on her
left wrist. Darn, she was fifteen minutes late.

She pushed her back against the seat and straightened
her arms, trying to stretch out some of the knotted muscles.
What a day! Not that it was all that different from most of
her days. What must it be like to have lots of leisure time,
to do just what you felt like doing when you felt like doing
it?

The answer shot back at her: boring. Letty grinned. She
might as well face it: She preferred an active life, sore
muscles and all.

Her attention shifted from her aching body to the lovely
trees lining the driveway. Driveway? What a laugh. This
was a private road leading into the two-hundred-acre estate
of Mr. and Mrs. Bartholemew Prindle. Despite her ex-

1

haustion, Letty felt a quick surge of excitement. She'd been wanting to see this house for years, and although she had thoroughly walked the grounds, she had not yet been inside.

The road curved left, and the moment she made the turn, her foot hit the brake. A covey of quail skittered across the even gravel in front of her. She watched the dainty fowl disappear into the brush, then took a few minutes to look around.

She was pleased to see that the entry lane had been kept natural-looking. The trees were properly thinned and pruned and the wild shrubbery cut back, but the impression was still one of a quiet country road. Good. That increased her chances for working compatibly with the Prindles. Her style of landscape architecture was to preserve and enhance the beauty of nature, and when a prospective client wanted something formal and structured, she referred them to someone else.

She hurriedly parked in front of the stately house, turned off the motor, grabbed her clipboard and her enormous purse, and headed for the front door. She was admitted by a pleasant, gray-haired housekeeper.

"Mr. and Mrs. Prindle are in the library, Mrs. Aldridge. They're expecting you."

"Thank you." She handed her lightweight jacket to the woman and followed her across the wide, stone-floored entrance hall to an oversized, intricately carved wooden door. The housekeeper knocked lightly before opening it.

"Mrs. Aldridge is here, Mr. Prindle."

A short, stocky man of about sixty with a ruddy face and a friendly smile got up from the dark red leather chair that had almost eclipsed him. He held his hand out as he approached her. "Mrs. Aldridge, how nice to meet you at last! We've had quite a time, haven't we, finding a date when we were all available. Meet my wife. Ellen, this is Letitia Aldridge."

Ellen Prindle was at least three inches taller than her husband, and at least twenty years his junior. She was also blond, buxom, and beautiful. Was this an example of what money could buy?

"I'm delighted to meet you, Mrs. Prindle."

"Please, just Ellen. Formality makes me nervous."

Letty's instant impression was that it would take a lot more than formality to make Ellen Prindle nervous. She turned her attention back to Ellen's husband.

"And I'd like you to meet Craig Sullivan, the owner of Sullivan Construction Company. Craig has agreed to do the engineering and the installation of the underground piping for the water runoffs, and to dig the pond."

The contractor in question started to rise from a leather chair that had its back to the door, effectively hiding him from Letty's view. "Oh, don't get up," she urged. "I'll just sit down so you can get back to your discussion. I'm sorry to be late. We were planting a seventy-foot tree and had a few placement problems."

She slipped into the chair next to the one occupied by Craig Sullivan, turning to offer him her hand as she did. "I'm glad to meet—" She stopped dead. Sparkling smoky-blue eyes peered at her from beneath the thickest lashes she had ever seen on man or woman. The look was lazily friendly but delivered about twelve thousand volts.

"Nice to meet you, Letitia Aldridge."

Totally flustered, Letty realized she had failed to connect with his outstretched hand. She moved to do so and found his grasp firm, businesslike, and unsettling. His slightly rough skin felt inordinately good against her somewhat callused palm.

". . . sketches to give you a rough idea of what we have in mind."

Damn. Mr. Prindle was speaking, and she had missed the first part of his sentence. Pull yourself together, Letitia, she ordered, forcing her concentration to the papers Mr. Prindle was spreading on the coffee table.

"As you can see, Craig has brought us a comprehensive plan of the pond layout and how the culvert will have to be redug. These"—his finger traced two double lines that met to become one—"are where the new pipes will be laid to handle the water runoff. Right now it runs down the back lawn and into the swamp, er, the pond. Craig, maybe you can explain to Mrs. Aldridge just what you're going to do, and then we can talk about the landscaping we want around the site."

Craig hitched himself forward in his chair, moving the plans over so Letty could see them more clearly. He leaned toward her, causing a disturbing fluctuation in her heartbeat. Letty pulled her chair closer to his—to see better, she told herself.

He placed his hand on the edge of the plan. It was square and deeply tanned, with long, sturdy fingers. A strong hand that looked as if it could handle any assignment. She impatiently pushed aside the one that instantly leaped to mind, aghast at her wayward imagination.

"As you can see, the pond itself won't be very large." He was soft-spoken, but his words were perfectly articulated. She moved nearer anyway—so she'd be sure not to miss anything. "I'm certain there are at least two springs there, so a good supply of water won't be a problem," he continued.

What *is* going to be a problem, she thought, is working with Craig Sullivan if I quiver every time I look at him. What would Duane say? It depressed her to realize that, even though she was engaged to Duane, he had never made her quiver. Not once. Oh dear, she'd just missed at least another whole sentence, and this was all information she had to know.

"The hydrologist has done a thorough study on the water tables and environmental effects. We'll have to go before the conservation committee for approval, since this is a wetlands area, but there should be no problem."

"Looks like so far it's a problem-free job."

The smoky gaze met hers, and deeply etched laugh lines appeared as he smiled.

Wouldn't you know, she thought. Beautiful white teeth.

The front one was a bit crooked, but somehow it didn't look like a flaw.

"No such thing as a problem-free job, I'm afraid." His voice had a delicious, velvety, Harry Belafonte quality.

Part of her mind followed the explanations he was giving, knowing she'd hear all this again at the conservation presentation, while the other part focused on his appearance. She was trying to determine what it was about him that had such an effect on her. She couldn't tell just how tall he was, of course, but he certainly wasn't a small man. And he looked very sturdy. If his construction company put him together, she thought whimsically, they sure did good work. He wore light-brown corduroys and a brown turtleneck under a pale gold chammy shirt. She wanted to run her hand over his arm to feel the texture—of the shirt, of course.

"This whole area would concern you." There was that jolting eye contact again. "If you take the job, that is." His gaze held hers, shaking her ironclad self-control. "I hope you will. I hear you're very good."

The unpredictable imp in her longed to challenge, "At what?" but Letty instantly realized that that sort of remark had no place in this conversation. "I'm extremely interested." She blinked. For some reason her vision seemed fogged. "From what Mr. Prindle tells me, the project sounds fascinating." Not to mention the participants, she mused before she could stop herself.

Mr. Prindle snickered happily. "You have no idea how long I've been pursuing Mrs. Aldridge!"

Letty's eyes flew to Craig, wondering if he had picked up any innuendo from that statement. She couldn't tell. Surely anyone would know that Bartholemew Prindle was not the sort of man she'd be interested in. She glanced quickly at Mrs. Prindle. On second thought, that might not be clear. What *was* clear was that Craig didn't seem to care one way or the other.

Letty was rapidly becoming impatient with herself. For a hard-headed businesswoman, she was behaving like a thorough ninny. Time to stop reacting to the handsome pond-digger and pay attention to what she was here for. "You were about to show me where the landscaping would be done," she prompted.

Craig looked at her again, his expression slightly changed, as though he had caught his first glimpse of the capable professional. He glanced over at Mr. Prindle. "Do you want to explain this part?"

"No, no, you're doing fine. As soon as you get to the gardens, I'll take over."

"Fine." Without lifting his eyes from the paper before him, Craig went on with his descriptions. "I'll be cleaning out and recutting a three-hundred-and-seventy-five-foot stream up this way." His finger followed the red line; her eyes followed his finger. "There's already one there, but the banks are so caved in and so much silt has filled it that it can no longer be effective in carrying water."

"Why is it called 'swale' on the plan?" Ellen Prindle interrupted, leaning over the papers in apparent fascination.

"That's a technical name for the depression that's made when we cut in for a stream or a creek or a runoff," Craig explained pleasantly.

"Will it feed right into the pond?" Letty queried, all business now.

"No. It'll be easier to keep the pond clean if all the water goes through an underground gravel bed first. That area tends to flood anyway, and it's the flow of ground water that turns a pond back into a swamp. There are a few plants and small trees along the creek and around the pond site that you might want to save. The cut will pretty much heal itself, but you'll want to be careful about plantings that might get invasive."

Letty felt a small flicker of irritation. "I'm always careful about anything invasive."

One side of his mouth curved up. "Sounds like a wise idea." His gaze lifted to hers and then away. "The hydrologist has some suggestions for pond plants; you can go over those with him. The area designated for the Oriental garden is at this curve of the swale, and the English garden here.

I understand the lawn will be brought down to the edge along the rest of the length." He stopped and leaned back, his sexy, still-water-runs-deep eyes regarding her with agreeable candor, his voice easy. "I guess the biggest challenge to the two of us will be staying out of each other's hair."

Oh, must we? She was ashamed of the thought the moment it entered her mind. She had pinpointed one thing about Craig Sullivan. He seemed completely oblivious to his enormous sensual appeal, which of course increased it immensely. If he was married, his wife must certainly look forward to having him come home!

If he was married. Why did that thought seem so awful? He had to be in his mid to late thirties; he was almost certainly married. After all, she was only thirty-five and she'd already been married, widowed, and was now engaged again.

The reminder of her engagement almost caught her by surprise. You *are* engaged, Letitia, she mentally reiterated, so obviously Mr. Sullivan's marital status has nothing to do with you in any case . . . darn it.

She pictured her conscience shaking its head at her in consternation. Her sexual antennae hadn't been this activated within memory. Actually, it was sort of fun to know she could still react so strongly. After all, as her thoroughly married friend Gwen often said, "I can still look at the menu; I just can't order."

"Why are you smiling?"

"What?"

Craig was studying her, his head tilted to one side. "You were smiling. I thought maybe I'd missed a joke."

She stared at him, aware that his voice was gently teasing. She hoped he couldn't read minds. "Oh! No, I, actually I was just thinking that staying out of each other's hair should be no problem." Fast thinking, Letty, she congratulated herself even as she feasted her eyes on his straight, silky brown hair.

Mr. Prindle crossed over to Letty's other side and drew

up a chair. "As Craig described, the Oriental garden I spoke to you about would fill this approximate area." He traced a pattern on the plan. "Ellen and I have cut out a number of pictures of things we like, but you're the expert. We've also accumulated a folder full of shots of English cottage gardens; we think one would fit in right down here,. where the nice gentle slope comes in." He looked at her anxiously. "I hope you don't mind having ready-made ideas thrown at you."

She held up her hand in a gesture of reassurance. "Not at all. I prefer working with people who have some concept of what they want."

"Then you'll take the job?"

She was startled by the suddenness of the eager question. The deference with which she was treated by so many of these extremely rich people never failed to amaze her. But, as she had learned, when homeowners began beautifying their land, they usually became deeply involved, not only aesthetically, but emotionally as well, and she became something akin to an earth priestess. "As I said, I'm certainly interested. But . . ." She hesitated. This was the part she always dreaded. "We haven't discussed the financial aspects of it yet."

"No problem!" Mr. Prindle fairly beamed at her. "You and I can sit down as soon as you're available. We can do it this evening if you'd like. I'm sure we'll reach an agreement, since I'm prepared to give in to all your demands in order to have you do the job."

"You could be opening yourself up for a first-rate swindle with a statement like that!" she warned playfully.

His smile still glowed. "I have no qualms whatever. You see, not only has your reputation as an excellent landscape architect preceded you, but also your reputation for scrupulous fairness."

Letty laughed. "Darn. Hoisted on my own petard. All right, I *will* take the job, and I'll also stay to go over the figures before I leave. It's better to have all that out of the way before we start."

"Wonderful! I suppose you and Craig will want to get together to talk about who does what."

Letty was aware that Craig had been sitting back in his chair, his luminous blue eyes seemingly recording the exchange. Now she suddenly noticed that she wasn't the only one riveted by his sensuality. Ellen Prindle was totally absorbed in Craig-watching.

The object of all this parched-lip attention remained relaxed and slightly remote. He glanced at Letty. "I guess we'd better work up a game plan. Is there any chance we could get together next Tuesday? I'm coming down from New Hampshire to see about another job. If I can do at least two in this area at the same time, it makes more sense to move the equipment."

"You live in New Hampshire?"

"Yep."

"That's quite a commute. Will you be staying here in the Boston area while you're doing the work?"

"No. I like to go home at night. So do my men."

She was engulfed in a wave of what could only be described as disappointment. "My," she remarked, trying to keep her tone light, "you must all have wonderful families to warrant that much commitment."

"Yes, most of my men are happily married and have kids. I have a dog and two cats who are very demanding."

"You're not married?" The question—and the undisguised amazement in which it was voiced—popped out of the mouth of the heretofore practically mute Ellen.

Craig gave her his lazy, sexy-as-all-hell smile. "No."

Ellen licked her lips. Letty silently reflected that Mr. Prindle would be wise to spend a lot of time at home while this job was being done. Aloud she said, "Tuesday will be fine. I'll arrange my other commitments around our meeting. We may find that we have to have a lot of contact by phone, since I'm sure it's a bit difficult to talk to you while you're running one of your machines."

"It seems it should be fairly cut and dried to me. I'll do my digging, and then you can do your planting."

"Oh, now wait a minute." Letty's back straightened. "I'll want to make a careful study of the site before any digging is done, and I'll have to be there to observe as the work progresses. If I'm to be responsible for the final results, I must have some say in each phase."

He didn't move a muscle—so how did he send off such vibrations of steely resolve? "I have a feeling," he said quietly, "that we just hit our first problem."

Mr. Prindle leaped up, alarm contorting his face. "Well! I'm sure we can all work together amicably. How about something to drink? The sun is well over the yardarm, or whatever that expression is. Mrs. Aldridge? What will you have?"

"Nothing at the moment, thank you."

Mr. Prindle looked even more apprehensive. He seemed to see his whole eagerly awaited project slipping through his fingers. "Craig?"

"A Coke would be nice."

"Just a Coke? Oh, that's right; you have quite a drive ahead of you."

"I don't drink much anyway. Like to keep my mind clear."

"Well! How commendable! I always admire someone with such strong willpower. Ellen, my dear, how about you?"

"Just a little ginger ale, darling."

Mr. Prindle looked amazed. "My, my. All this temperance all of a sudden. It seems I'll have to drink alone."

Letty watched Ellen watching Craig. Mr. Prindle didn't understand female strategy, she thought. Suddenly tired of the scenario, Letty said, "I've changed my mind. I'll join you. Scotch on the rocks, please."

When her eyes shifted, they ran right into the steady gaze of the blue-eyed pond-digger. No question about it, they were sending a direct challenge. His dark eyebrows lifted slightly. Was this to be war? She lifted her own eyebrows in response to the challenge. You may be cute as all get-out, she thought, but don't mess with me. As an antagonist,

I can be a tough cookie. That one side of his mouth curved up again. Ye gods, he *could* read minds! Okay, so we're both tough cookies. This is going to be a very interesting job!

With her ginger ale held in one manicured hand, Ellen Prindle stood and crossed to the ottoman that matched the leather chair occupied by Craig. With silky grace she lowered herself onto it, leaning forward to bombard him with a three-pronged attack: two large breasts and an eyelids-lowered sensual smile. "I can hardly wait to see your machine in action," she purred.

Letty choked on her scotch. She watched the corners of Craig's mouth twitch. He's dying to respond to that one in an appropriate way, she guessed, but he's probably too much of a gentleman. She was right.

"It *is* interesting to watch a pond being dug." He played it straight, only the twinkle in his eye betraying a touch of . . . amusement? Letty hoped so. Or interest? She hoped not.

"When do you think you'll be doing it?" Was Ellen actually batting her eyes? She was!

"Oh, I'd say around the middle of July. I understand we go before the conservation board on June twenty-sixth, and I can work this job in before a big site-development project I have coming up in Maine."

"Oh, good. Then it'll be easy to watch you. I spend most of my time out by the pool in the summer. The view will be perfect."

Which view, Letty mentally groused. I bet there'll be a pretty spectacular one of E. Prindle in an itty-bitty bikini. Suddenly Craig's answer struck her with full force. "Hey!" She almost jumped at her own utterance. "Sorry, I didn't mean to yell, but July would be a terrible time to do this. There are a lot of plants along that swale and around the pond site that must be moved, and most of them shouldn't be disturbed until at least the latter part of August."

"Why can't you move the plants out of the way, then put them where you want them later? It's the end of May;

it should be safe to move them in June, right?" Craig challenged.

"Wrong! Many of these grow wild, including beautiful groups of wild azaleas, and to completely replant them twice in one season would be far too much of a shock to them."

"And just what am I supposed to do with my project in Maine?"

She itched to tell him exactly what he could do with his project in Maine, but instead she took a sip of her drink, attempting to control her unruly temper. Her late husband used to lament that it was too bad he couldn't have the beautiful redhead without the flyaway temper. "I don't want to be unreasonable, Mr. Sullivan . . ."

"Craig."

"Craig. But after all, plants, like dogs and cats, are very demanding." That won her a point, a small smile. She tried to force her own hazel eyes to twinkle instead of snap, which she was sure they were doing. She also tried to spread a sugar coating over the edge of her voice. "Maybe you could move the Maine job forward to July."

"They won't be ready for me in July." He didn't look angry, just interested, as though he was curious about what her next move would be.

"I see. Don't you have any other jobs?" The sugar coating wasn't sticking; the edge was too sharp.

"I have a great many jobs, Mrs. Aldridge."

"Letty."

"Letty. All carefully scheduled."

"I see. And is this schedule totally inflexible?"

"Nothing's *totally* inflexible."

They stared at each other, measuring the entrenchments, stocking the ammunition.

This time Ellen interceded. "Why don't the two of you work out all these little details on Tuesday? Anything you decide will be just fine with me. The sunbathing is good right through September."

Dear heaven, Letty thought, I'm going to barf. One thing

was crystal clear: If the conflict got too heavy and one of them had to go, if Ellen had anything to say about it, Letty would bet it would *not* be Craig Sullivan.

"We'll try to work something out." Craig had settled back into his nice-guy demeanor. She'd have to be careful with him. People who could keep their cool almost always won an argument.

"Yes." Having finished her drink much too fast, Letty felt a little woozy. "Is it possible for us to meet toward the end of the day, so I can get some work done?"

"Sure. Maybe you and your husband could join me for dinner. I hear there's a good Italian restaurant over in Natick."

"I'm a widow, Craig."

"I'm sorry."

"That's all right. I'll see you Tuesday, then."

"Fine." Those come-hither eyes were reassessing her. Was it her imagination, or might he be registering the fact that she was a woman as well as a landscape architect?

She was suddenly sorry she had rushed straight over from the tree-planting job without stopping to shower and change out of her jeans and heavy shirt and rubber L.L. Bean boots. She also looked a heck of a lot better with her red hair combed out instead of knotted at the back of her head, and with a touch of makeup. Letty! her mind scolded. Remember, you're engaged.

To her dismay, Craig stood and extended his hand to Mr. Prindle. "I think I'll hit the road. It's a long drive home, and I have to be in Portland, Maine, tomorrow morning at seven. I'll see you soon after the conservation meeting on the twenty-sixth."

The openly aroused Ellen had also risen and was standing as close to Craig as she could, Letty assessed, without causing him to pitch back into the chair. "I'm certainly looking forward to this whole affair," Ellen purred. It was hard to tell if her remarks were planned or simply the result of too much space between her ears.

"I'm looking forward to it, too."

What did he mean by that, and wasn't he holding her hand a shade too long? And was it any of her business? No, but since when had that ever made any difference?

She got up and waited for Craig to get around to paying some attention to her. She tried to measure his height by stretching up to her full five-feet-five. About five-eleven, she'd guess. When he did look at her, she mentally assigned herself the task of going home and writing *This is just a business relationship* fifty times.

Craig held out his hand to her. She was almost afraid to take it. "I'll see you on Tuesday evening. I'm sure we can find a way to work together without eating each other alive."

Letty gulped and forced a friendly smile. "No problem."

They all laughed, and Craig left on a wave of good cheer. As soon as he walked out, the room seemed drab, less richly textured, to Letty. She was getting almost as besotted as Ellen Prindle!

Mr. Prindle offered to refresh her drink, which she hastily declined, and the three of them went over the ideas for the two gardens and the plantings around the pond and along the swale. She was surprised and pleased to discover that Ellen Prindle was very informed and equally vocal about the project.

By the time Letty left, she had built a good rapport with both Prindles. And she'd decided it wasn't fair to condemn Ellen for ogling Craig when she'd been guilty of the same thing herself. Hoping that a good thought canceled a covetous one, she headed for home.

Letty always enjoyed turning into her own driveway. It in no way equaled the Prindles' in length or neatness, nor did it lead to such a grandiose dwelling, but it did resemble a country lane. In this case the dirt tracks had lost most of their gravel and underbrush swiped the side of the car, but it felt like coming home, and that was good.

She pulled the car into the garage and climbed out, surprised at her weariness. Hard work didn't usually affect her so. It must have been her response to Craig Sullivan that was so tiring, she surmised, chuckling at her excursion into fantasy.

She gave the matter some serious consideration while she unlocked the door, really trying to remember the last time she had experienced an instantaneous reaction even close to the one Craig had caused. If it had *ever* happened before, it was beyond memory. Despite her teenage crush on her husband, John, they had practically grown up together, so there had never really been a "first encounter" like this one. And Duane? She had known him for years, and her first impression of him had been . . . well, first impressions weren't to be trusted anyway.

As soon as she stepped inside she was greeted by her faithful friend, who stood patiently in the front hall. "Hi, Pudge. How was your day?" She gave him a scratch behind the ear. "Do anything exciting or unusual?"

"Meow." Pudge blinked his great, round, bright blue eyes, then turned to lead her to his favorite room, the kitchen.

"You know, Pudge, your eyes are almost the same color as the man's I met today, although his had a little more gray in them. And, no offense, but I have to confess to you that his were sexier. Not that I don't love you, you understand, but hairy males have just never turned me on."

Pudge rubbed against her ankle, then sat at her feet, staring up at her as if to ask, "And how do you know he's not hairy?"

"All right, all right, so I don't know. But really, Pudge"— she took a can of cat food out of the cupboard and wedged it into the electric can opener—"no one could be as hairy as you are."

She was right, of course. Pudge was a flame-point Himalayan with thick bone-white, sienna-marked hair that was close to three inches long.

"You're a wonderful friend," she assured him as she set his dinner on the floor in front of him. "In fact, you are the most faithful of companions. Even when you can't be with me personally, you send along some of your hair as a memento." To emphasize the point, she picked a few long strands off her navy-blue jacket.

"Letty!" The call came from the front door. "Are you here?"

"Yes, Dad, in the kitchen, feeding my cat."

"First things first, I see. You must have just come home." Her father strode into the room and stooped to give Pudge a friendly pat. The cat paused long enough to look up and utter a polite "Meow" before returning to his meal. Her father then leaned forward to give Letty a kiss on the cheek.

"You should talk about first things first," she chided. "I notice who always gets your first greeting around here."

"Yes, well, I hate to get on the wrong side of Pudge. I'm not entirely sure what he is. He's the only animal I've ever known who sits in the middle of a conversation and comments at just the right times."

"I know what you mean. Dad, how nice to see you! Did you come over to invite me out to dinner, or did you drop by for a less worthy reason?"

"Actually, I dropped by to borrow your Rototiller, but I'd be happy to take you out to dinner. We'd have to go someplace informal, because, as you can see, I'm far from dressed up." He regarded her for a moment, then added, "But at that, I look more presentable than you do."

"Now don't get snide. I've been working all day."

"You work too hard."

"You're late with that remark, Dad. You usually say that right after you say hello to Pudge and kiss me on the cheek."

"I'm right, in any case. It's eight o'clock, Letty, and I daresay you left the house this morning at the crack of dawn as usual. What *are* you trying to do?"

"It's called 'making a living,' Daddy dear."

"Humph. I'd say more like shortening your life-span. Besides, you don't need to make a living. You have more than an adequate nest egg."

"Maybe I want to be rich."

"That's easy. All you have to do is wait for me to die."

She stared at him. He was only kidding with her, but she hated to even entertain the thought that her father was mortal. Trying to regain a light tone, she said, "I can't be expected to wait that long. With your lineage, I'll be seventy-five and no longer interested in amassing a fortune."

"Seriously, honey, why do you push yourself so? I could understand it for a few years after John's accident. It helped you forget, I'm sure. But that was eight years ago, Letty. Surely you don't need quite so much candle-burning anymore."

"Look who's sermonizing! Pardon me for bringing it up, but you are of what is often considered to be retirement age, and you never miss a day at the office."

"That's different. Lawyers don't retire; they just become part of the molding on the office paneling. Don't change the subject. What you need is an interesting, full-of-hell man to use up at least part of that incredible energy."

"I have a man, Father. I have Duane."

"No comment."

"Now, Dad, just because Duane isn't a big, macho hunk . . ."

"Duane is a wimp, and you know it. He lets you lead him around by the nose."

"You brought me up to be a leader."

"Oh, dear heaven, deliver me! If there's anything a parent hates, it's having his misbegotten good intentions tossed in his teeth. Go take a shower and get the smudge off your face, at least. I'd like to think your mother and I bred a bit of culture into you. I certainly didn't envision my dainty little girl growing up to spend her adulthood mucking about in the mud."

"Mother taught manners. You taught drive. And she didn't last long enough into my life to have equal say."

"You should have learned *something* by the time you were fifteen!"

"I did. To go after what I want."

"It seems to me that brings us full circle. What *do* you want?"

"To landscape everything. Today the northeast, tomorrow the world!"

"Letty . . ." Her father seemed to be trying hard to make his rugged, handsome face glower. "Go, before I give you that spanking you've needed for so many years."

"You mean the one you've been threatening me with since I was five?"

"Exactly."

"I'm going, I'm going." But she took time to give her father a tight hug, which was warmly returned. They had been each other's bulwarks through the losses of those other two people who had completed their worlds. Letty loved and admired her father. He was a big man in every respect, tall and husky and generous and kind. Also immensely successful. They really were two of a kind. Neither needed the money; both needed the work. She kissed him on the cheek and headed for the bath. "I'll be right back. Don't get lonesome!"

"Never fear. Pudge and I will discuss the events of the day."

Letty finished blow-drying her short crop of red curls and touching up her lipstick. She glanced at her watch. Ha! It had only taken her twenty minutes, and her dad was always teasing her about being slow getting dressed. Just as she started downstairs, the phone rang. "Could you get that, Dad?" she called.

"Sure."

When she entered the living room, her father was holding the phone, one eyebrow raised. "It's a Mr. Craig Sullivan," he said.

She felt a telltale flush rise to her cheeks. She tried to turn away as she took the phone, but her father hadn't missed a thing. "Ta-ta, Duane," he murmured.

Shooting him as fierce a look as she could muster, she tried for a businesslike "Hello," but her voice cracked.

- 2 -

"HELLO, LETITIA. WE forgot to set a time."

"A time? What do you mean?" She could feel her cheeks burning and see her father smiling.

"For Tuesday."

"Oh! Of course. Tuesday! What time is convenient for you?"

"I thought you were planning this around *your* schedule."

Was he baiting her? Whatever he said seemed to do remarkable things to her blood pressure.

One more glance at her Cheshire-cat grinning father was enough to impel her to rein in her emotions. "I have a feeling, Mr. Craig Sullivan, that you speak softly and carry a big stick." There! A good, stern tone.

There was a long pause. Long enough for the double entendre in her remark to hit her right between the eyes. Oh please, she prayed, don't let him pick it up! When he did speak, she knew beyond a doubt that nothing had es-

19

caped him. She could almost see the tilted smile. But his reply was, as she had already come to expect, gentlemanly. "Don't worry about it. I'd never strike a lady."

She remembered a few of Ellen Prindle's remarks and his courteous answers. He must have scars from biting his tongue. "Any time after four would work well for me. If that's a problem for you, I could try to shove some of my work over to Wednesday."

"No, that's fine. That other job I'm looking at is over in Weston. That will give me time to go talk to those people. Suppose I pick you up at six. Would that suit you?"

"That would suit me fine, but won't it make you rather late getting home?"

"I'll get a note from my dog."

"The cats have no say?"

"The dog is the current president of their union. They hold elections every six months."

"Must make for a remarkably democratic household."

"Well, not quite. The one who never gets a vote is me."

"You poor thing." She knew she was grinning like a fool. "You sound terribly put-upon."

"I am. Beleaguered."

"Bull."

"Please, Mrs. Aldridge. My dog is monitoring this call. She's easily shocked."

"Your dog is a she?"

"Yes. Why do you sound so surprised? Lots of dogs are."

She was actually giggling. "Well, I'm sorry to end this fascinating exchange on animal politics, but my father is waiting to take me to dinner. At this rate we may both starve. I'll see you at six Tuesday evening."

"Fine."

"Good night."

"Where?"

She stared at the receiver as if it was a puzzle she hadn't figured out. "Where what?"

"Where do you live?"

Good grief, she must sound retarded. Play it cool, Letty. Pretend you're not an air-head. "Oh, you're a detail person."

"Yep."

"I live in Sherborn. Not far from the Prindles, as a matter of fact. Geographically, that is."

His low chuckle raised goose bumps on her arm. And other places. "Do you have an address?"

"Yes." She gave him the address. "It's on the mailbox—if the mailbox is standing on Tuesday."

"Does your mailbox have a habit of lying down?"

She was giggling again. "Only when the local boys have a wild night on the town. The biggie here is mailbox destruction."

"Poor mailboxes. Such defenseless little critters, too. Maybe you should give me directions, including how to find your house if the mailbox is a current casualty."

She gave him directions, said good night again, hung up, and faced her father. "All right, Caleb Marsh, wipe that grin off your face. You look like Pudge did after he watched *Alice in Wonderland* on TV."

Caleb had little success banishing his grin. "Just who, may I ask, is Craig Sullivan?"

"He owns a construction company. Site construction. You know, heavy equipment that moves earth around."

"Looked like he was doing a little earth moving."

"Dad . . ." She glared at him. As usual, it had no effect.

"What exactly is the purpose of this Tuesday rendezvous with said earth-mover?"

"He's digging the pond on the Prindle job, as well as doing a number of other site improvements. We have to coordinate our efforts."

"Sounds interesting." The grin broadened. "And what does Mr. Sullivan look like?"

"A mud fence."

"Letty, never in all my days, which have been numerous, have I seen that kind of expression on the face of a woman talking to a mud fence."

"All right, all right! So he's rather nice-looking. What

difference does it make? He's simply a man I'm going to be working with for a short period of time. I spend most of my working hours with men. So big deal!"

Caleb took the trench coat she handed him and helped her into it, a speculative gleam still lighting his eyes. "Don't get huffy. I just sort of wondered why your face was flushed and your eyes were sparkling and you were stuttering, that's all."

"Dad! You're exaggerating!

"No I'm not. You looked just like a woman in love."

"Now that's the silliest thing I've ever heard. Despite what you men like to believe, women do *not* fall in love at first sight—not past their teen years, at least."

"Bull."

"Dad!" She stamped her foot. "Are you going to take me to dinner or not? All the restaurants will be closed pretty soon."

His eyes widened in innocence. "Let's go. I'm not the one holding up this operation." As they walked out the door he noted, "Funny. I haven't seen you stamp your foot since you were a teenager."

"Oh hush, wise guy."

Despite the fact that Letty's calendar was claustrophobic from overscheduling, Tuesday seemed to take forever to arrive. When it finally did, she awoke with a Christmas-morning exhilaration, telling herself innumerable lies about the cause: that it was a particularly bright, lovely spring morning; that the small dinner party she had attended with Duane the night before had been particularly cheerful—actually it was she who'd been particularly cheerful, as Duane had kept commenting; that being pursued by the Prindles for a job of that scope was a real feather in her cap. She just plain refused to acknowledge the smart-aleck inner voice that kept singsonging, "Dinner with Craig, dinner with Craig!"

The day itself sped by. She had designed the landscaping for a new library in Dover, and someone had donated funds for a first-rate job. They had started the actual planting on Monday morning, and by Tuesday afternoon at three-thirty the three workers, with Letty's constant supervision and frequent participation, had planted nine rhododendrons, eleven azaleas, three crab apple trees, fifteen junipers, seven cotoneasters, nine hostas, three mountain laurels, fifteen Purity irises, and four flats of vinca minor. It was beautiful, and she was exhausted.

She mumbled at herself all the way home, irritated in turn with having worked hard enough to be so tired and with worrying about being tired. She'd just finish up the evening's business as quickly as possible, excuse herself right after dinner, and have Craig bring her home early for a good night's sleep.

The minute she stepped under the hot shower she began to feel better—certainly lighter—as about four layers of dirt washed away. She scrubbed her head, lathering her hair three times before she was sure all the grime was gone. Then she submitted to a long ordeal with the fingernail brush, going after every elusive speck of dirt. She was far from a picture-book-dainty female gardener.

She took unaccustomed pains with her appearance, applying mascara and eyebrow pencil and even trying the three graduated tones of eye shadow she'd bought on impulse and hadn't even opened as yet. Her blow-dried hair looked especially tousled, so she searched for her curling iron, finally found it buried deep in a closet, and fussed with it until her hair curled softly around her face.

Next on the agenda was deciding what to wear. There was that lovely blue-gray dress her dad had given her for Christmas that she hadn't even worn yet . . . Come on, she reminded herself, this is supposed to be casual. She settled for a flattering wool skirt in a plaid of muted greens and a moss-green lamb's-wool sweater that emphasized her slimness and nicely rounded bosom. When she was dressed, she dabbed on some perfume, then assessed herself in the mirror.

Darn. She *looked* like a woman who had taken pains

with her appearance. With a touch of impatience, she kicked the high-heeled pumps back into the closet and slipped her feet into some comfortable flats, then deliberately ran her fingers through her carefully coiffed hair.

Pudge, who had been lying on the bed watching the whole routine, blinked once and rolled over, turning his back to her.

"Ah, come on, Pudge. Don't be mad at me for leaving you tonight. I won't be long. And I'm not going out with Duane." Duane openly disdained cats, long-haired cats in particular. "I'm going out with a man who has two cats of his own." She thought it expedient not to mention the d-o-g. Pudge rolled over to face her, looking interested. Clearly he shared her father's opinion of Duane. Sometimes she wondered why she . . . But that was silly. She loved Duane. At least she liked him a lot, and he was good company.

Duane and his wife had been friends of hers and John's during the last few years of their marriage. His wife had died of cancer three years after John's death, and Duane had, in a natural, uncomplicated way, become Letty's escort. He had seemed like a panacea after her ordeal with John.

Bland is best? Unbidden, the question popped into her mind. "Yes!" she answered aloud, shutting out all the little mental detractors. "It's certainly better than what came before!"

After all, she and Duane shared many friends, both enjoyed an occasional evening at the theater, and both belonged to the same country club, where they sometimes joined other couples for a game of golf. It was . . . well, it was a very convenient relationship. It had seemed sensible, when he proposed for the third time right after Christmas, to say yes. He kept pressing her to set a marriage date, but Letty was far too busy to think about that. It was the beginning of planting season.

She checked her watch. Ye gods, only five-thirty, and she was all ready. That must be a record. She actually had a few free moments to look over the new catalogue from Wesbank Nursery. Just as she started downstairs, trying to avoid stepping on Pudge, who was sticking close to her heels, the doorbell rang. "Aha, good thing I'm ready. He's early."

She opened the door, saying, "So you finished ahead of schedule, too . . ." There stood Duane, a big bouquet of mixed spring flowers in his hand. He persisted in bringing her flowers, even though she had dropped several broad hints that, since she worked with plants all day, coming home and arranging bouquets was not her favorite activity. "Why, Duane, what a surprise."

"Hi, Letty. You seemed so full of spring cheer last night that I thought I'd bring you some more." He stepped inside and stopped, staring at her with obvious surprise. "Gosh, you look terrific. Did we have a date I forgot, I hope?"

"No." Why did she feel so flustered? Her date with Craig was a perfectly legitimate business appointment, nothing unusual. That it *felt* a bit unusual was her business! "I've got an appointment with the man who's to dig the Prindles' pond. It seemed convenient to talk over dinner, so neither of us would have to lose any time from work."

"Do you have to get that duded up for a pond-digger?"

He made the occupation sound inferior. Duane was a banker. Why did her father's assessment "damned stuffed shirt" come to mind? She opened her mouth, about to defend Craig's trade, then closed it just in time. "I was filthy when I got home, and it felt good to get clean and 'duded up.' Sometimes I worry about looking like Tugboat Annie."

"You? Not a chance. You're too beautiful for that."

For some strange reason Duane's compliments often made her feel uncomfortable, as if she should put her finger beneath her chin, curtsy, and say, "Thank you, kind sir." She was saved from any response by the doorbell sounding again. "Busy place," she commented in what she hoped was an insouciant tone.

This time she kept her mouth shut as she opened the door. It was a good thing. It was her father.

"Hi, Titia." It was the pet name he used for her when he knew he was on shaky ground. The ferocious glare she sent him must have made him fear the earth-mover was at work. "I just stopped by to return your Rototiller."

She looked him straight in the eye. "You just *happened* to pick five forty-five on Tuesday evening to return my Rototiller?"

"What else?" He gave her a Little Orphan Annie, in-nocent-as-could-be stare. If he weren't her father, she'd hit him over the head. "Why, Duane, what are you doing here?" he said, clearly trying to get himself off the hook.

"I dropped by to give Letty some flowers and see if she'd like to go out for a bite to eat. It looks like I'm too late. She's got a date with some workman."

Caleb nodded knowingly. "Titia's always mingling with that sort. Why, she's even been known to get her hands dirty." He glanced pointedly at Duane's spotless, manicured hands.

The sarcasm passed right over Duane's head. It was amazing, Letty noted, how many things did.

She looked at her watch again and then around her at Caleb, Duane—who was still clutching the flowers—and Pudge, who had joined the group and was sitting close to Caleb's left foot. "Craig's going to feel as if he's the guest speaker at a convention. Why don't you guys go home now and come back another time. This man is rather shy. I doubt he's going to want to be inspected by a banker, a lawyer, and a sulking cat."

"Oh!" Duane's voice took on a phony heartiness. "There's Pudge. Hi there, Pudge." He bent over to pat the cat.

Pudge edged behind Caleb and hissed.

"That cat doesn't like me."

"Well, why would he, Duane? You're always saying mean things about him."

"Yes, but I bring him catnip mice and *act* friendly. Cats can't understand what people *say*."

"That one can," Caleb commented, stooping down to give his furry friend a reassuring scratch.

The doorbell rang once more.

"Oh poopydink!" Letty almost stamped her foot again but caught herself in time, though not quickly enough to avoid her father's knowing smirk. This was far from the cool reception she had envisioned for Craig.

With ill-concealed irritation she swung the door open. He looked wonderful. Right there in front of the assembled throng she could feel her knees go weak. "Hello there!" Talk about phony heartiness! "Come in."

Craig stepped in, barely fitting into the crowded entry hall. His sturdy, masculine frame dominated the area, making Duane's slight form seem a trifle frail. He even overpowered Caleb's solid presence. "Looks like a convention," he commented. "I hope I'm not expected to speak." Startled glances bounced among the other three.

Letty laughed, beginning to appreciate the humor in the situation. "As a matter of fact, we just took a vote on that, and you are."

He grinned at her, turning her weak knees to wobbly. "Sorry, I must decline. Public speaking is not my forte." He turned to Caleb. "I'm Craig Sullivan. If you're not Letty's father, you should be. She has your eyes."

Caleb grasped the outstretched hand. "I guess she does at that. I'm glad I don't have her temper." The two men shook hands vigorously, the instant rapport visible.

Craig then introduced himself to Duane. The handshake was not as hearty, the rapport nonexistent. Letty watched the whole procedure with numb astonishment, realizing that Craig had, with complete ease, taken the social initiative and handled it with unselfconscious grace. Duane looked a little stunned and also slightly foolish, balancing his bouquet in his left hand so he could shake with his right.

At that moment Pudge walked into the middle of the forest of legs, lay down, and stretched out flat on his back, tilting his head to peer up at them with his wide blue eyes.

"I'll be damned," Caleb snorted. "Look at that! Pudge has decided to be adorable."

Craig looked down at the cat and laughed out loud. "Hey, that's great. He's learned the yoga dead pose!" He stooped down and, sitting on his heels, addressed the outstretched animal. "How do you do, Pudge. I'm Craig."

Pudge rolled over and, with catly dignity, sat squarely in front of Craig and emitted a meow in reply. Craig rubbed the cat's head, and a loud, responding purr rattled the air.

"For crying out loud," Duane sputtered. "That stupid animal won't come near me, and look at it! Any minute now it's going to offer a paw to be shaken!"

Craig picked up the compliant fur ball and stood, still rubbing Pudge's head. In a quiet, level inflection he said, "A cat can sense antagonism, and it offends his dignity. Cats are very bright and very perceptive."

Caleb looked from cat to Craig. "If that's not your cat," he remarked, "he should be. He's got your eyes." The two men roared, and Letty could have sworn Pudge was laughing, too. The one somber face in the crowd belonged to her fiancé.

With a mixture of loyalty and pity, she crossed to Duane and took the flowers out of his hand. "I'll run in and put these in water. Thanks for bringing them. That was sweet. Then we'd better go. This was not slated to be a fashionably late dinner."

Craig's gaze met hers. "Are we *all* going to dinner?" The question was put in a friendly, interested manner. She wished he seemed more disturbed by the prospect.

"No. This contingent just gathered by happenstance. Our decisions about the Prindle property do not have to be made by committee vote." She dashed to the kitchen, grabbed a jar out of the cupboard, filled it with water, and stuck in the flowers, making no attempt to shape the display. Grabbing her trench coat off the back of the chair where she had thrown it earlier, she reentered the front hall.

Craig was leaning languidly against the wall, stroking the long white hair of the noisily purring cat that still lay cradled in one arm. They were the only ones there. His bluegrass eyes lifted to hers. "Your dad and your friend said to tell you good-bye."

"Not my friend, my fiancé." Aha! He *could* register surprise!

"You're engaged to him?"

"What's the matter with that?"

"Nothing. Nothing at all." He placed Pudge gently on the chair against the wall. "Just didn't seem your type, that's all."

"And why not?" Why did she feel so defensive?

He studied her face, and one brown eyebrow raised ever so slightly. "Seemed a little... submissive. But then, it's none of my business." He took her coat and held it for her. "One thing, though..."

"What's that?" Why was she snapping?

"Can't he be your fiancé and your friend at the same time?"

"I didn't say he wasn't!"

"Funny, I thought you had."

"In fact, he's far more a friend than a—" She stopped dead, appalled at what had almost come out of her mouth.

Craig opened the door and stood aside for her, watching her with knowing eyes. He made no comment, simply closing the door and waiting for her to lock it and set the burglar alarm. He led the way to a new-looking dark green pickup truck with SULLIVAN CONSTRUCTION CO. neatly stenciled on the door. "Sorry you have to ride in the truck. I had to bring some supplies down with me."

"I'm used to riding in trucks. I do it all the time."

"That's right, I suppose you do."

"Are we going to the Italian restaurant?"

He gave her a hand up into the cab and closed the door before walking around to climb in beside her. "What do you prefer? I hear there's a good steak house over on Route 1 and a good Chinese place in the same area."

"I'm sort of a meat-and-potatoes woman myself."

His sidelong glance brushed over her face as he turned the ignition key. "You're a hot ticket, that's what you are."

A flow of warming blood surged through her, heels to forehead. She wished he'd just turn off the motor, follow her back into the house and up the stairs, and... "Did you get the job in Weston?" Her voice was a little shaky, but not bad.

"Looks like it." As he guided the truck carefully down the rutted driveway, Letty found the scraping of branches against both sides embarrassing. Gardener, clean up thine own garden, her mind carped. Also thine own act. "We'll have to straighten out just when we're doing the Prindle job, so I'll know whether I can work anyone else in at the same time. Moving bulldozers around is expensive. Moving the crane is very expensive."

"Is the crane what you use to dig?"

"It's what I'll use to dig the pond. Also what I'd use for the job in Weston, if I take it. That guy has a dam on his property that's breaking down and needs to be rebuilt. I told him the first step in a job that big is to check with the Army Corps of Engineers to make sure the water volume isn't great enough to fall within their jurisdiction. I think he's safe, but I tangled with those fellows once before, and once was enough."

"I'm learning all sorts of new things. I have to admit it would never occur to me that a homeowner would have to get involved with the Army to do work on his own property."

"When you start messing with water tables, you'd be surprised how many people get involved."

"Did you do the layout for the Prindle pond, or did the hydrologist do it?"

"The hydrologist, Dr. Fish."

"You're kidding!"

"No, that's his name. The fish just couldn't stay out of water."

"You had to say it, didn't you."

"Yeah." He glanced over and grinned. "Before you did."

Letty leaned back against the seat, feeling relaxed and happy. Craig clearly had a knack for putting people at ease. It seemed he also had a knack for turning women on. She wondered if he knew it, or if he was as oblivious to his appeal as he seemed to be with both her and Ellen Prindle. In any case, she'd have to be on guard not to betray her unruly reaction to him. That would undermine her effectiveness in their working relationship. It would also make her more vulnerable than she cared to be with any man.

A disturbing thought crept into her mind. Could that be why she had attached herself so firmly to Duane? Because she didn't want any emotional hassles? No. Duane was a considerate, kind man who would make her a good husband. The turbulence she had experienced during her first marriage was enough for one lifetime. Her work now used most of her energy; she didn't have a lot left over for demanding relationships.

Soon they were pulling into the parking lot of the restaurant. "You know," she commented, "I just realized I'm starved. We had so much to get done today that I never took time for lunch."

"No wonder you stay so nice and slim."

She stared at his profile as he parked the truck. It was a pleasant surprise that he noticed what she looked like. "I'll probably embarrass you when we get inside. I eat like a truckdriver."

"Or a crane operator?"

She grinned. "Is this going to turn into a competition, too?"

"You mean you think other things will?"

"I think we're edging toward shaky ground. Maybe we should avoid it until after dinner. I don't want my appetite spoiled."

"Meat and potatoes coming up." He got out of the truck and walked around to help her.

It was funny; his manners were so good they were almost courtly, yet there was nothing patronizing about him. A remarkable man, Craig Sullivan.

As they walked side by side to the entrance, he remarked, "By the way, it would take a lot more than your overeating to embarrass me."

"Oh really? What would it take?"

He arched an eyebrow at her as she stepped past him into the restaurant. "I have a feeling anything I suggested might be used against me."

"You make me sound dangerous."

"I think you may be."

Letty watched him as he spoke to the hostess. He wore navy-blue slacks, a white shirt under a light blue crew-neck sweater, and a beige corduroy jacket. How could anyone look so cuddly at the same time he exuded so much masculinity? She was shaken by the magnitude of his attraction. Lust was a totally unfamiliar visitor to her mind, but it was there now, hiding between otherwise well-disciplined brain cells. It frightened her, and very few things did. Craig was soft-spoken, low-key, and gentle, and he packed an unbelievably potent sexual wallop. Talk about dangerous! *He* should be posted.

They were seated in a private corner that was illuminated only by the flicker of a single candle on the table. The light accented Craig's firm, square jaw. He sipped a Coke while he studied the menu. Letty sipped her scotch while she studied him. The cleft in his chin was so deep she bet she could hide the tip of her little finger in it . . . or the tip of her tongue. She pulled her eyes away from him and focused them on the menu, wishing the words printed there would quit swimming around and settle down.

"What would you like?"

She jumped, startled by the question. Should she tell him? Of course not. "I'll have a filet, medium rare, and a baked potato."

"What a surprise." The smiling eyes that met hers were darkened to midnight blue by the dim light. The lashes were so long they cast shadows above the straight, well-shaped nose. She wanted to touch the one crooked tooth that gleamed in its bright company. She wanted to touch . . . "Do you want a salad?"

"Yes, please. With the house dressing."

Craig placed the order, then directed his full attention to her. It was dreadfully unnerving. "How long have you been a widow?"

"Eight years."

"And how long were you married?"

"Five years."

"You must have married awfully young."

"I was twenty-two." She cocked her head at him. "That makes me twenty-nine now, right?"

"No question." The waitress put the salads in front of them. "You certainly don't look any older than that."

"You surprise me."

"Why?"

"I had the distinct impression, until a short time ago, that you hadn't even noticed my appearance."

"You were wrong. When I met you at the Prindles' you had your hair all pushed back and a smudge on your chin."

"Thanks. I needed that."

"Tonight you look sparkly clean, your hair is shiny and curly, and you're beautiful."

She couldn't move her eyes from his. She was swimming in twin blue thick-fringed ponds, and the water was warm and caressing and very, very deep. Were there undertows in ponds? Yes. Definitely. "Craig?"

"What is it, Letty?"

He made the crisp, no-nonsense "Letty" sound musical, like "Ophelia," or "Miranda." Imagining how it would sound whispered in her ear, with his mouth pressed against her cheeks, she felt a sharp contraction beneath the napkin on her lap. "You're a very appealing man. Why aren't you married?"

"I wish you'd stopped at the first half of that."

"Why? Don't you like to talk about marriage?"

"I was supposed to be married last October. It was canceled."

"Why?"

"The bride left me just before we got to the altar."

Letty couldn't imagine any woman in her right mind walking out on Craig. "She must have been nuts." She wanted to reach across the table and wipe away the pain on his face. "What happened?"

"Oh, it was probably pretty understandable. I started my own business about seven years ago, and it's just now starting to pay off. She was real interested until she saw how I plow most of my profits back into the company. She met a guy who had his money in a bank instead of heavy equipment."

"I'm sorry."

"I'm not. It was a narrow escape from what would have been a mistake. I'm over the hurt; it's the anger that hangs on."

So it was anger she saw in his expression, in the hard set of the jaw. Hurt, anger. Sometimes it was one and the same thing. She knew. "There are other women in the world," she offered. He didn't respond.

Her gaze clung to his compelling face. Craig Sullivan in his casual, self-confident guise was alluring. Craig Sullivan looking vulnerable was irresistible. She'd better change the subject. "How did you get started in construction work?"

"I got an after-school job with an old friend of my father's when I was about fifteen. His name was Tony Bellini. He hired me as an oiler."

"What's an oiler?"

"You keep the bucket on the crane oiled and polished, and the other equipment clean. It's the bottom peon job, and you work your fanny off. I was driving a bulldozer before I finished high school."

"Did you stay with Tony Bellini?"

"Off and on. For years I operated a wrecking crane in Boston. Then I got drafted."

"You were in the Vietnam War."

"Only in a manner of speaking. One of my officers found out I could handle all those machines, so they put me in charge of a huge building project on one of the Army bases up in Maine. And there I stayed for my whole two years of service."

"Weren't you lucky!"

"Yes. I was."

"So then what? Did you go back to construction right away?"

"I worked part time and went to school part time. Got my engineering degree. Then Tony retired, and I bought the big crane from him and started my own company."

"Pretty gutsy."

"Some people said insane. I hocked my whole future to do it. Been doing that ever since."

"What made you decide on that course?"

"Well, I didn't want to run a bulldozer all my life. Construction companies are almost always family affairs, generation to generation. Tony didn't have any sons, so he taught me a lot more than he would have otherwise."

"Are most of them Italian?"

"Italian and Irish. I'm Irish."

"With a name like Sullivan? I never would have guessed! So you decided you'd prefer going into business for yourself to running a bulldozer?"

"That's about it."

"How much equipment do you have?"

"Well, I have two wide-track bulldozers—those are low to the ground so the weight is more evenly distributed, with fewer pounds per square foot. One big dozer and one small. There's a rubber-tired loader with a scoop in front, and two end dumps."

"End dumps?"

"You know, rock trucks. They're huge off-road vehicles. And we have three trailers for lugging all this around, and four pick-ups, and—are you still interested, or are you sorry you asked?"

"I'm very interested."

"Aside from that, let's see, a couple of welding trucks for repair work, electric and gas pumps . . . and odds and ends."

"That *is* a huge investment."

"Yep. But last year I spent two hundred and fifty thousand dollars to rent machines I didn't have. So at the end of the year I bought two. It'll pay off in the long run."

"How many men do you have?"

"My brother works with me. He's the administration whiz, keeps everything straight. Then there's another engineer and a job supervisor and a project manager and three or four full-time working foremen. The rest we hire by the job."

"Pretty impressive. And are you making your fortune yet?"

"No, but at least the bills get paid."

The waitress placed two large steaks in front of them. Their delicious aroma wafted up to Letty's nose, temporarily taking her mind off the subject at hand. "Oh boy, does this look good."

"Time to stop talking and start eating." Craig picked up his knife and fork and cut a piece of the succulent steak. Before putting it into his mouth he looked at her and added, "And then we'd better get to the real subject of the evening: namely, who's going to have control of what on the Prindle job."

Their eyes met across the table. The competition was about to begin.

- 3 -

LETTY CLOSED HER eyes and savored her first bite of the cooked-to-perfection steak. She often forgot to eat during the day; it was easy to get caught up in the rush of her overscheduled life.

"I can see what you meant; you do like to eat, don't you?"

She opened her eyes but continued her unabashed munching. "Mmm-hmm."

"Letty, we've talked a lot about me. How about you? Do you like your work?"

She swallowed and nodded. "Love it. I can't imagine anything I'd rather do. Every time I start a new job I get excited all over again."

"When did you decide you wanted to be a landscape architect?"

She looked over at him and narrowed her eyes. "What are you doing, Mr. Sullivan, delaying the confrontation?"

37

"Yes, until after dinner. If I'm going to war, I want to go with a full stomach."

"Good idea. By the way, do you mind if I have a glass of red wine with my meal?"

"Of course not. Why would I mind?"

"Well, to be honest, I wasn't sure whether you just don't drink, can't drink, or disapprove of drinking. Since I already had a scotch, I didn't want to put myself in too bad a light."

"Does that mean my opinion of you carries some importance?"

She wasn't about to tell him how much importance his opinion of her carried. "Certainly it does. Besides, when one is plotting a confrontation, one concentrates on displaying strengths, not weaknesses."

"You're doing well. I haven't spotted any weaknesses yet."

"Never fear, you will."

Craig signaled the waitress and ordered a glass of wine for Letty. "I don't drink because I have too many friends who reached the 'can't' stage. A couple of them had a tough time between wet and dry. Watching them took all the enjoyment out of it for me. But no, I don't disapprove."

"You know, Craig, it's too bad we're planning to go to war, because I like you."

"The feeling is mutual. Maybe we'll be able to carry off this whole job in peaceful coexistence."

"Why not? We're both after the same result. There's just a little matter of timing."

"Ah!" He stopped her with his hand. "After dinner, remember?"

"Okay."

"You were going to tell me how your career started."

"Do you mind if I interrupt with chewing?"

"Not at all."

"I planted my first flower garden when I was six. Dad and Mom both loved to garden, and they taught my sister and me the rudiments of how things grow."

"You have a sister?"

"Yes. Six years older. She's great, but unfortunately she and her husband have lived in England for the last three years. His job took them there. She got married when she was only nineteen, much to my parents' dismay, but luckily it worked out well."

"What about your mother?"

"Mom caught pneumonia when I was fifteen, just a year and a half after Jill got married. Everyone expected Mom to recover, but she didn't."

"Must have been rough on your dad."

"Just awful. On both of us. Jill, too, of course, but she was at least slightly insulated by her new marriage and being so in love."

"I think I'd enjoy getting to know your father."

"That feeling appeared to be mutual. He obviously took to you right away. Quite a contrast with his reaction to my fiancé. He's less than enchanted by Duane."

"Really? How about you? Are you enchanted by Duane?"

"I'm engaged to him."

"You didn't answer the question."

How could she say yes at the same time she was looking across the table at that face, wanting to push the dark brown hair off his forehead and then tangle her fingers in it and bring those full, firm lips to hers? She barely knew him; it was indecent to yearn for him like this.

"Maybe I'd better retreat to a previous question. I decided to go into landscaping when I was about ten. I designed, dug, and prepared the ground and planted an herb garden in our backyard. It was a huge success. I believe I was prouder of that than anything else I've ever done. It was the first thing that was all mine, and everyone raved about it."

"Is it still there?"

"Yes."

"Would you show it to me sometime?"

She looked up at him, thinking, *How about right now?*

*It's nice and dark out there. You couldn't see much, but
there's a nice soft patch of lamb's ears.* "Sure. We can take
a break while we're at the Prindles'. It's not far from there."

"Good. They had been eating steadily between verbal
exchanges and had nearly finished. "How are you doing?
Want to have coffee and dessert, or fight first?"

Letty's mood was definitely mellow. There was no quar-
reling with the fact that there were a lot of things she'd
rather do with Craig Sullivan than fight. "Might as well talk
it out. As you said, there aren't all that many actual reasons
for disagreement. Basically, you'll do the digging, and I'll
do the planting. The piping and the underground culvert are
strictly your business. The potential danger areas are the
cut of the swale and the pond—and the timing."

"I looked for time flexibility, but there isn't any. It'll
have to be the first week of July or next spring. Unless of
course we could sneak the equipment in without letting the
conservation committee know. Then I could do it next week."

She stared at him in amazement. "Is that a serious sug-
gestion?"

"No."

"Well, I'm relieved to hear that!"

"I'm glad I can say something you're relieved to hear."

"Ah. So in that sturdy chest beats a heart of gold."

"Indeed."

"It just happens to be encased in a veneer of cast iron."

"My schedule was set two months ago. Evidently you
only decided to take this job the other night."

She forced her fingers to stop their drumming on the
edge of the table. "Am I being told, politely but pointedly,
that had I wanted this done at another time I should have
made up my mind sooner?"

"You got it."

"So much for your heart of gold. Now, the other little
matter . . ."

He was leaning back now, his arms crossed in front of
him, his eyelids drooping slightly, a corner of his mouth
curved. His waiting-game pose, she suspected. "The other

little matter, like whether you're going to try to tell me how to dig my pond?"

"*Your* pond! I thought that future body of water was to belong to the Prindles."

"As long as I'm digging, it's my pond. When I finish digging, as far as I'm concerned, it's up for grabs. You can arm-wrestle them for it if you'd like."

"That's outrageous! They're paying you to do a job, and they're paying me to do a job. We don't *own* the territory, even while we work on it! As for my involvement in what you do, part of the responsibility I have is to use my expert eye—and to be honest, it *is* expert—to envision what the entire area will look like when it's done. That pond will be the focal point, and the shape of the swale coming down to it is of vital importance. I know exactly how those gardens should fit into the curves, but I need the curves in the right places."

"I'd say you already have the curves in the right places."

She plunked her elbows on the table and leaned forward. "Now that kind of a remark in this kind of discussion really ticks me off!"

The lips curved up a bit farther. "I figured it would."

"Dirty pool, Mr. Sullivan!"

"Letty." His voice didn't escalate one single decibel. "You point out which plants you want, and I'll try to get them out before I start the major excavation. If they have to be dug by hand, your men can do it. But as soon as that's taken care of, *I* will do what I do better than anyone else on the eastern seaboard."

"Pretty cocky, aren't you?"

"I know my capabilities, just as you know yours."

Letty started her mental counting; it was an exercise she had developed to control her temper. It did have a way of getting out of hand at the most inopportune times. What he had said about the schedule was reasonable. He had planned on the Prindle job long before she had, and there was no malice in his teasing, so why was she getting so irritated? Maybe there really weren't any disagreements here beyond the bad timing. "All right, let's review the facts. Will the creek be kept the way it is? That's what appears on the plan."

"Yes. As far as possible."

"What does that mean?"

"It means it's next to impossible to guarantee that we'll be able to maintain the exact configuration of a three-hundred-and-eighty-foot creek bed until we actually dig it. But I will attempt to do so."

She sighed, relaxing a few tense muscles. "Then that should be okay. And the oval pond will be fine, so maybe we can sign a truce before the outbreak of the war." Feeling greatly relieved, she smiled at him. "If I take extra care moving the plants, I can undoubtedly save most of them." This was beginning to look like a piece of cake.

"The pond won't be oval; it'll be kidney-shaped."

She stared at him in disbelief. "What are you talking about? It was oval on the plan!"

"I told Bart Prindle I wasn't sure that was best when I first looked at it, and he told me to use my own judgment."

"But that spot *needs* an oval pond! Why on earth would you want to make it kidney-shaped?"

"Because it will look larger from the house, because it will fit into the terrain better, and because I might be able to incorporate four natural underground springs instead of only two."

"Why can't you just make it larger if you want to tap the springs? I've already made the preliminary sketches of an oval pond, and it's lovely! It would offset the shape of the garden at the top of the rise perfectly!"

"The pond will be kidney-shaped, and it'll look terrific."

"The way it *looks* is *my* business. *Digging* it correctly is *your* business."

"Letty, I told you before: I'll dig the pond, and you do the planting. It will be kidney-shaped. I suggest you revise your sketches."

She was experiencing a slow burn, and this one had

nothing to do with lust. "You are a pigheaded man!"

"Ah, ah! Your temper is showing. But you're cute when you're mad." As her face reddened, his grin expanded. "I know, that kind of remark really ticks you off."

"You'd better believe it!"

"Letty, you'll like the pond. I've done a lot of them. I know what I'm talking about. You don't always have to win, do you?"

"Winning is sure way ahead of losing!"

His voice became even softer. "Just what is it you're so afraid of losing, and what is it you're so intent upon winning?"

"I know my business, and I tell you that pond would look better oval!"

"You're wrong."

She sat very still, staring at her empty plate, fighting to curtail the rise of fury inside. She had always had a temper— her family used to kid her about being a typical redhead— but she had, with fierce determination, learned to control it . . . at least most of the time. She had to admit that she often went home and kicked doorjambs and threw pillows. But even there she had disciplined herself against throwing anything breakable. She'd become so mild that Pudge now slept right through her tantrums.

It was just . . . well, there was something about Craig that was awakening sleeping tigers. Maybe he was right. Maybe she should let him do his work by himself and stick to her own job. That way she could keep her distance. It was beginning to feel like the only safe thing to do.

"How are you doing?"

"What?"

"Your face was almost as red as your hair. I wondered if you were winning the battle or if I should dive for cover."

Propping her elbow on the table, she rested her chin in her hand and scrutinized him with faint uneasiness. "You give me the creepiest feeling; you seem to be able to read my mind."

He chuckled. "It isn't all that difficult. When steam starts to come out of one's ears, the natural assumption is that the person is upset."

She added the other hand to help sustain the weight of her increasingly heavy chin. "You're going to be a real problem to me."

His eyes widened. "Oh? And why is that?"

"You stay so calm. A person with a shotgun mouth like mine always loses an argument to calmness."

"I don't want to argue with you, Letty."

Her head rose slowly from its improvised support, her eyes imprisoned by his gleaming, hypnotic gaze. What *did* he want? Did his blood run faster when he looked at her? Did he ache to reach across and trace the outline of her face with his finger? Did he wonder, and want to know, how her skin would feel against his? She longed but didn't dare to ask.

The waitress put a steaming pot of coffee on the table between them. Letty stared at it, transfixed, as it visually metamorphosed into a square, vapor-emitting container. Pandora's box. She mustn't, mustn't open it. Her life was exactly the way she wanted it to be: structured, controlled, safe. Filled with the joy of her work, a home that was also a retreat, family, friends, fiancé. But what about when the fiancé became a husband? She shook her head to clear it. What on earth was all this about? She was making a mountain out of a pond-digger!

Her eyes were pulled back to his steady gaze. Admit it, Letty, her mind cautioned, what you see before you is no molehill.

Without looking away from her he asked, "Do you want dessert?"

Do I ever! her capricious mind retorted. "No, thank you. I think I need to go home to bed." She fought the startled flush that edged toward her face. "I'm bushed."

"That's right, you've had a tiring day."

It was nothing compared to the evening, she thought. "If

you want dessert, I'm sure I can stay awake a while longer."

He shook his head. "Bed does sound good, doesn't it?"

The hyacinth eyes beckoned her, conjuring up a mental picture of her wide, chaste bed, made unchaste by this alluring man . . .

She shoved her chair back, almost knocking it over. "Will you excuse me for a minute? I must go in search of the ladies' room."

He stood as she fled in the direction of the lobby. Was she mistaken, or had she heard him murmur "Chicken" as she left?

The ride back to her house was made in comparative silence, the weighted air of weariness seeming to encircle both of them. The truck reached the end of the bumpy driveway, and Craig pulled up in front of the door. Leaving the motor running and the brake on, he got out to open Letty's door for her.

She sat still and waited for him. She was perfectly capable, naturally, of opening her own door. She was capable of *driving* a truck and loading and unloading its cargo of shrubs and trees and bales of peat moss. But Craig made her femininity assert itself. Besides, she wanted the excuse to touch his hand.

When he helped her from the truck, his fingers held hers for just a few short moments longer than was necessary. He walked her to the door and waited while she fumbled for her keys, deactivated the alarm, and unlocked the door. "I'll wait until you go in and check around."

She didn't protest as he stepped into the entryway and stood while she went into the living room, turned on a couple of lights, and dutifully made a quick check of the upstairs. She never gave a thought to possible intruders, and she didn't now. The only thought in her head was how nice it felt to know he was in her house.

When she returned she announced, "All clear. No bogeymen."

He nodded. "I guess you're safe and sound."

She didn't feel safe and sound; she felt shaken and besieged. "Yes."

"I enjoyed our evening." His enchanting smile lit up the dim room. "Even the confrontation."

"That's because you won."

"Did I?" The smile left his face. "Why don't I feel as if I did?" He reached out his hand, and very slowly and gently, cupped the back of her neck and drew her to him.

She offered no resistance: there was none in her to call upon. She saw those longed-for lips coming closer, then felt their achingly sweet touch on hers. The kiss was brief, undemanding, and shook her to the balls of her feet.

Craig drew back mere inches and looked at her. "I was right," he said. "You're dangerous." With that he removed his hand and turned to step back through the open door. Looking over his shoulder, he said, "Good night, Letitia. Pleasant dreams."

Immobilized, she stood and listened to the crunch of his tires on the driveway, the acceleration of the motor as he pulled out onto the quiet street. Then she closed the door and locked it.

As she turned to walk into the living room to shut off the lights, she almost stepped on Pudge, who sat silently at the edge of the rug, regarding her with wide-blue-eyed interest. She tried to ignore him as she clicked off the lamp. Finally she snarled, "All right, smarty-paws, quit smirking!" and scooped him into her arms to carry him upstairs with her.

He gave her chin a loving lick and settled into a rumbling purr. "Inscrutable cat, my foot," she muttered. "I know what you're thinking . . . and I'm afraid you're right."

She was absolutely sure Craig would call. She had a speech all rehearsed. She would be kind but firm about the fact that she was committed to another man, and she would remind him of the unreliability of fleeting moments of attraction. She would take care not to injure his ego while she outlined strict rules for future behavior. She would patiently list all the reasons they would be incompatible and smile with tender understanding at his disappointment.

He didn't call, and she thought she would lose her mind.

How could he be such an inconsiderate slob, getting her emotions all riled up, then not even having the decency to phone! It reinforced her conviction that mere sex appeal in a man was no basis for considering a serious relationship with him. And adding likable, intelligent, and enterprising to the list still didn't make it long enough to offset the years of steady, reliable companionship she had accumulated with Duane.

Luckily, the month of June was an all-out cruncher for someone in her business. She was doing the landscaping for a brand-new house with three acres, a swimming pool, and barren surrounding grounds completely devoid of trees. As a counter challenge, her other major job for the month was to rescue a hundred-and-fifty-year-old house that sat in the midst of a pine grove so dense that the roof was suffering from a severe case of mold and the lawn had long since browned over and refused to try anymore. Fortunately, the new owners, the Bakers, hadn't even blinked when she told them the first step had to be the removal of forty-five trees. On top of these two large projects were several lesser ones—additions to existing gardens and planning sessions for jobs she would tackle in the fall.

In the midst of it all she spent a great deal of time working up the plans for the Prindle property. That was a real challenge, a made-in-heaven opportunity for a landscape architect. She had been honest with the Prindles, letting them know she had done only one other complete Japanese garden. Nonetheless, they both seemed to trust her judgment, and she was having a wonderful time researching, sketching, consulting with specialists in Oriental plantings—including the helpful group at the Arnold Arboretum near Boston—and dashing off whenever she had a spare minute to look at established gardens.

The English cottage garden was a natural for her. It was

one of her favorite styles of planting, and although she didn't consider herself an expert on perennials, she had a good friend who was, and they often collaborated. But she already knew exactly what the layout should be and could picture the end result in her mind.

As long as she could keep her mind off Craig Sullivan she was fine, and by the middle of June she had stretched those spans of mental discipline to as long as five minutes at a time, give or take a few seconds.

Her exposure to Craig had not improved her relationship with Duane. It hadn't had any major negative effect, but she found herself getting restless in Duane's company and mentally nit-picking about some of his habits. Even though she was irritated by her own reaction, she seemed unable to do very much about it.

On an unseasonably hot June twenty-second Letty was squatting on her heels at the just-built-house site, directing the placement of a twelve-foot tree. It had rained heavily the night before, and what had been flat, dry ground by the new swimming pool was now a sea of squishy mud. The three men who worked with Letty were planting the eleven hemlocks and yews of varying heights she had selected to serve as a screen between the pool and the neighbors. Although the Frazier house sat on three acres, the only logical place to build it had been within sight of the house on the left. Since in this neighborhood tall fences were considered unsightly and unfriendly, part of Letty's job was to place trees and shrubs where they would eventually grow to provide privacy.

"Over to the left, Jim," she called, "and just slightly forward. Good! Now, about a one-quarter turn to the right, so we get the best face. That's it! Dig the hole and set it. Sam, that one will be toward the front, to your left. No, over a good three feet; the pendula sargenti will go on this end so it can be seen. Len, will you bring the two carolinianas with the skimpy sides over? I think they'll work just fine alternated with the nigras."

She was trying to get the visual effect from a seated

position by the pool, but she finally had to stand and stretch her legs. When all the evergreens were placed, she would carefully view them from every direction before the men filled in the holes. She went to drag the garden hose over so the holes could be filled with water as soon as they were all dug and the loam and peat moss mixed in. Plenty of water was a must.

She glanced down and grinned. Her feet looked like two movable mud pies. After turning on the water, she leaned over to take a drink out of the end of the hose. Gosh, it was hot outside! After a moment's hesitation, she bent forward and let the cool water run over her head. The sound of laughter from the three workers was immediate.

"Hey, Letty!" Len yelled. "How about getting that hose up here so the rest of us can cool off?"

She uncoiled a kink in the rubber tube and tugged it to the planting site, where the men followed her lead. Since they were all bare chested, they watered themselves more thoroughly; then Jim stuck the end of the hose into the first hole.

Jim Blake was Letty's unofficial chief assistant. He kidded her about being his "mentor," occasionally adding adjectives like "aged" or "venerable." And she enjoyed instructing him. He was bright, hardworking, and determined. At the age of twenty he had already acquired more knowledge in the field than any of the other men who did work for her, many of whom had been at it for ten or fifteen years. Jim attended night school and was saving toward the day he could go to college full time to get his degree. Letty knew he'd be a fine landscape architect one day; he was already a darn good gardener.

After watering he walked over to confer with her. "Those blue-rug junipers are all pot-bound. Do you want to distress them while we finish putting in the hemlocks? That way I bet we could get them all planted by four o'clock. Len and Sam want to quit then so they can get to the Cape for the weekend."

"Sure. Why don't you get the rest of the hemlocks positioned, then I can double-check them and have the men fill the holes while you place these. I'll have them all ready for you."

He smiled. "Okay. Thanks."

She watched him rejoin the others, knowing that the thanks was for the increasing trust she'd been putting in his judgment. It was amazing, the pleasure to be had from passing along one's expertise, especially to a particularly apt pupil.

She got a piece of the burlap that had been used to ball the trees and spread it out to sit on. There were seven junipers to be prepared. After extracting the first from its plastic container, she took her curved, three-pronged weeding tool and began the job of "distressing." The plants had been in containers long enough to become pot-bound, the dirt hardened and the roots so matted they couldn't get free to grow as they should. When Letty finished vigorously raking the entire circumference of the base, she set the juniper aside and reached for the next.

It was Friday, and that evening she and Duane were going to a cocktail party and then on to a dinner party. It sounded exhausting. Duane loved big parties, with lots of people to talk to about golf and football and the latest Dow Jones figures. Letty liked most of the people they would see tonight; she just preferred them in smaller doses. She enjoyed getting together with two or three other couples, so they could really *talk* to each other. Although she did play a little golf herself, she flatly refused to go to after-tournament parties, where the contestants endlessly described each and every stroke for each and every hole. Duane usually went to those gatherings alone. But fair was fair. She belonged to several horticultural organizations whose members often got together and talked endlessly about growing things. Duane had endured those affairs until she'd ended his misery by assuring him she didn't mind going alone.

She sat back for a moment, her gardening fork poised above another pot-bound juniper. "What on earth will Duane and I talk to each other about when we're married?" she muttered. Why hadn't she thought of that before? Since their schedules were so jammed, they only got together once or twice a week. Well, being honest, she acknowledged that *her* schedule was jammed and Duane had filled his in with other activities over the years they'd been seeing each other. What did their relationship really consist of, and why hadn't she truly examined it before?

"How are you doing?" At the question she looked up to see Jim's long legs beside her. He squatted next to her and held out his hand for the forked tool. "The hemlocks are placed, so I'll finish this while you take a look."

"Okey-dokey."

"Okey-dokey! Jeez, give me a break!"

"Don't like that expression?" She grinned at him. "How about 'gee whillikers, you betcha'?"

"Oh yeah, that's much better. Don't try those on Len and Sam, or you'll get drenched again without planning on it."

Letty gave him a mock salute as she headed up the rise toward the other two. Unlike some of the other men, Jim's language was fairly mild, but she had heard just about everything in her years of working. It had become almost a game for Letty to come up with the corniest, most innocuous expressions she could muster to toss into the middle of some of the stormy swearing sessions—for instance, when they were trying to dig through the usual New England soil, namely, solid rock, or forced to finish a job in the middle of a rainstorm. And she had some real zingers, such as "jeepers crow!" or "dad-gummit!" or "oh pshaw!" She had to admit, however, that there were times when her "redhead" psyche took over, and she added to the blue hue of the prevailing mood.

They did finish by four, successfully completing the work scheduled for the week. As Letty drove home, she vowed that the next car she bought would have air conditioning. She was dirty, sticky with sweat, and dreadfully uncomfortable. It was a good thing she didn't have to see anyone on the way home. She must be a sight!

She sighed with relief as she swung into her familiar driveway. Boy, would that shower feel good! When she came to the end of the drive, she almost ran into the back of a pickup truck that was parked on the right. As she edged around it, she saw the name SULLIVAN on the door. "Oh no!" she wailed. "Not now!"

There was no time even to push her straggly hair out of her eyes before Craig approached the car. How could he possibly look so fresh and scrubbed at the end of a working day? "Hi." He gave her a friendly smile. Did he even remember that he'd kissed her? "I like your hairdo."

She got out of the car with as much dignity as she could muster, which, she feared, was not considerable. "Thanks. It's a new style, called garden-hose fluff."

"Nice." Didn't he have a less lethal smile? Something with fangs or green teeth, perhaps?

"You look pretty spiffy. Did you take the day off, or have you gotten an office job?"

"Would you find that more acceptable?"

She stared at him in amazement. "Acceptable? For what? I doubt you'd dig a very good pond from behind a desk! And don't try to tell me you worry about my opinion of your career; that would worry *me*."

"Why?"

"Because, judging from my very brief experience with you, it would mean you're after something."

The smile went from enticing to mesmerizing. "Of course I'm after something. The only question is, will I get it?"

How did one deal with a remark like that? Throw caution to the winds and invite him upstairs to her bed, risking rejection as well as a shattered future? Or search for a cutsie-pie answer to let them both off the hook? "I guess we're all after something. At the moment, what I'm after is a shower." Innocuous had won the day.

He pulled a thick envelope out of his pocket. "Dr. Fish sent me a catalogue with circled suggestions about what should go in the pond when it's done. You should look it over and see what you think."

She took the envelope, giving it an inordinate amount of attention. "What sort of things are we talking about?"

"Underwater plants and all sorts of squiggly things. I didn't want to order them until you had a chance to review the choices."

"Excuse my former assessment—you *are* all heart. Under this somber exterior is a woman who adores squiggly things." She looked up at him, suddenly overwhelmed with a need to shove aside this foolish banter. "Craig..."

"Yes?"

"Are you in a hurry? Would you like to come in for a cold drink?" Her heart began to pump; it was so hard to extend an invitation when you really cared whether or not it was accepted.

He stared down at the ground for at least twenty heartbeats, then raised his eyes to hers. "Letty..." He stopped and looked at her, as though torn by deciding what to reply. "You're...well...the term used to be 'spoken for.' And I am a man who doesn't believe in invading someone else's territory."

Those blue-gray passion inciters gazed at her—longingly? she wondered. She hoped so.

"If you're really engaged to that...to Duane, then we'd better confine our relationship to business." He pushed a damp, dirty strand of hair off her forehead. "If that's possible."

Within seconds he was gone, leaving her with a catalogue of available amoebas, plankton, freshwater mollusks—and a blood-pumping system that had run amok.

Very slowly she opened her door and greeted Pudge. The ball was in her court, and no matter which way she returned it, she could lose. Lose what? Some mythical game of life? Anyway, she sure did hate to lose. She'd already lost in two professional encounters with this man. "Careful, Letty old sock. Strike three and you're out!" she muttered.

Damn. When had everything become so complicated? The answer was disarmingly clear: the afternoon at the Prindles' when she'd turned to say "How do you do" to Craig Sullivan.

- *4* -

DUANE WAS DEPRESSINGLY cheerful that night. He had taken the afternoon off for a round of golf, and he spent the half hour it took to get to the cocktail party describing each and every shot for each and every hole. "Boy! Eighty-three! Not bad for a weekend golfer, eh, Letty?"

"That's wonderful, Duane."

"Why do I get the impression you're less than enthused?"

"I'm sorry. But you know I have trouble really getting into who did or didn't sink a six-foot putt."

He snuck a quick glance at her as he drove. "It seems to me you're too absorbed in your work lately, Letty. Nothing else raises any interest. It's not like you to let yourself get that one-tracked. Is something wrong? One of the jobs fouling up?"

"No." She stared down at her clenched hands. "I don't know what it is. I just feel more tense and unsettled than usual. The mood will shake out, I'm sure."

He pulled off the road at the end of a long row of parked cars. "Here we are." He turned to her, his expression of concern visible even in the dim illumination of the street light. "Letty, when do you get to that big job? You know, the one you've done so many plans for?"

"The Prindles'? The one with the pond?"

"Yes. Why can't you take a week off right after you finish that? We could get married and go on a honeymoon. Someplace quiet and relaxing."

Letty stared at him through the dusk, glad her expression was clothed in semidarkness. Married. That was the logical conclusion to an engagement. So why did she immediately want to barrage him with reasons why she couldn't possibly marry him at that time? Or any other, for that matter?

Damn. It was terrible when your own mind started asking you tough questions; it became very hard to sidestep them. "Well, that's a possibility. Let me think about it." Poor Duane. It would be difficult to miss the lack of enthusiasm in her voice. Why didn't he just tell her to buzz off? Because he was too patient for that, she answered herself. He was too patient, period.

As they walked up the long driveway toward the loud laughter, loud voices, and loud music, Letty's mind rolled the question over and over. Did she want to marry Duane, or had she simply drifted into an easy relationship that was controllable and not too demanding? Had she drifted into it or sought it? In many ways it was just the kind of relationship she envisioned, the kind she needed after the awful end to her stormy marriage.

Duane was nice to be with. He was considerate and kind and—admit it, Letty, your father is right—easily led. She could work Duane into her schedule with no difficulty, because he allowed that. Well, if it satisfied both of them, why not? Every marriage didn't have to be based on passionate desire. In fact many of them would probably turn out better if they weren't. It was just . . . well, if she married Duane, she'd obviously have to go to bed with him, and the object couldn't *always* be sleep!

So far Duane hadn't pressured her much about sex. Of course she'd made it clear that she clung to old-fashioned principles: sex *after* marriage. Unfortunately, just a couple of exposures to a blue-eyed pond-digger had been enough to put the lie to that premise. So what now, Letty? her nosy mind demanded.

Luckily they had entered the house and been caught up in the party. She could postpone answering questions a while longer.

By the time she got home that night and chastely kissed— and left—Duane at the door, she was in a foul mood. There had been an extraordinary number of smokers at the cocktail party, which had given her a headache; the dinner, at their second destination, had followed another cocktail more-than-hour, which had delayed the appearance of any food until past eleven o'clock; and the food, when it finally *was* served, was far too rich to be consumed at that hour. All she wanted now was to take some aspirin for her throbbing head and get some sleep.

But once she lay in the safe haven of her bed, her relentless mind began to plague her again.

The plain truth was that her settled, carefully programmed emotions had been shaken, and she hadn't the foggiest notion what to do about it. She now had reason to believe that something more personal could come of her business relationship with Craig. But did she want anything to come of it?

She had, over the past several years, learned to curb her passionate nature, even forgetting for long periods that she had one. And that had worked pretty darn well for her, shielding her from unwanted onslaughts of emotion. She'd better stick to her plans: Get the Prindle job behind her, forget the gleam in those blue-water eyes, marry Duane, and let her life settle back into the easy rut it was in before. Damn! There had to be a better word than *rut*. She stroked the soft fur of the purring cat curled up beside her.

"Oh, Pudge," she whispered. "Wanting someone isn't all that great. It just gets you all churned up inside, and most of the time the wanting isn't equal . . . it's more on one side than the other."

Pudge stood, nudged her nose with his a couple of times in his own special cat kiss, and lay down propped against her leg.

"I've had both kinds," she continued, sure that Pudge didn't mind listening. "I wanted more than my husband could give, and now Duane wants far more than I can give. Do you suppose there's such a thing as an equal relationship?"

Pudge tilted his head back and blinked once, then closed his eyes. Clearly he knew an unanswerable question when he heard it. Letty turned out the light and closed her own eyes. Pudge had life management under control. If there was such a thing as reincarnation, she'd put in her bid to be a pampered house cat.

When Letty walked into the town house at three minutes to eight on June twenty-sixth, she felt far more in charge of her emotions than she had a few nights before. She had firmly decided that allowing a handsome stranger to waltz in and disrupt her perfectly acceptable life was just plain foolish. Thus fortified against the impact of said handsome stranger, she entered the room where the conservation committee held its meetings.

Craig wasn't there. She felt a dramatic letdown, followed closely by impatience with the feeling. What dips we women are, she thought. I bet men aren't this irrational, despite all our talk of equality!

"Hi, Letty!" Dan Walker, the chairman of the committee, gave her a friendly wave and reached over to pull out a chair for her. The other three members present also greeted her cheerfully. She was well known to all of them. Well known and, she hoped, well liked.

"Hi, guys. What's first on your agenda?"

"The Prindle job, if everyone shows up on time." Jess Barnes, a lean, work-and-time-weathered man who had been born and raised in the town and devoted countless hours of service to it, handed her a sheet listing matters to be presented to the board that evening. "Looks like quite an undertaking, Letty. The Prindles were lucky to get you. You'll do it right for a fair price. If anyone else got a load of that layout, they'd sure as hell tuck it to them with one whopper of a bill."

Letty touched his arm, a gesture of friendship and appreciation for his vote of confidence. "It should be beautiful when it's done, Jess. The Prindles have good taste. No neon lights."

They all laughed. The reference to neon lights had become a standard with the group since the night, three years before, when a plan had been presented by a man who wanted to excavate a bog and fill it with concrete, complete with fountains and statuary and intricate lighting that twinkled on and off like simulated stars. The plan had been rejected, but the story had been recounted and enlarged upon many times.

If there had been a chiming clock in the room, Craig would have arrived on the eighth dong. As soon as he appeared in the doorway, Letty's heart began to flutter—much to her annoyance. He paused just inside until he was joined by a short, nervous-looking man with a large briefcase. When they were both in the room, Craig introduced himself and Dr. Fish to the men on the board. When he reached Letty, he said, "Hi, Letty. Meet Dr. Fish." The twinkle in his eye reminded her of the corny "fish out of water" joke.

"Hello, Dr. Fish. I'm glad to meet you."

The hydrologist smiled, jerked his head in acknowledgment, and crossed hurriedly to the other side of the room, where he pulled forward a large easel and began to arrange some charts he'd brought.

Craig took one of the chairs that were against the wall and placed it next to Letty's, sitting closer than was good for her blood pressure. He watched Dr. Fish for a minute, then leaned over and whispered, "Very nervous man, Dr.

Fish. He should learn to relax, maybe take up a hobby."

"Like swimming?" Letty slid it in quickly, then grinned smugly.

"Got me," he admitted. "I'll have to be on my toes to get the worst-joke award with you around."

The meeting was called to order, and Dan officially called for the presentation of the Prindle project. Dr. Fish handed out fully bound, twenty-eight-page reports to each of the board members. "All the facts I will be discussing are in this report," he said. "These charts are to show you the full extent of the changes planned and their impact on the surrounding wetlands."

Jess leafed through the extensive booklet. "Good Lord!" he blurted. "Are these people putting in a small pond or an ocean?"

Dr. Fish, who had missed the comment, continued. "This will be a combined wildlife and amenity pond of not over one-half acre. It will be on private land and will not be visible to any neighbors."

He covered the alterations to the wetlands, stressing that the overall effect would be advantageous for flood control, vegetation increase, and fish population. "It will also serve as a nesting area for ducks and geese, as well as a watering station for other wildlife."

Letty took cursory notes concerning the pipe layouts and underground culverts but activated her pen considerably when Dr. Fish described the existing ecologically appropriate plants. She listed the ones she would want to replant: swamp dewberry, highbush blueberry, Virginia creeper, northern arrowwood, sweet pepperbush, the grasses, the ferns, and the mosses.

Craig looked over at her pad. "Don't want to transplant the poison ivy?"

"Just where you'll be sitting to have your lunch," she whispered back.

Dr. Fish described the soils found at different depths in test holes, and the consequences of ten-year to one-hundred-

year rain levels. He assured them that bales of hay would
be placed at the inlet and outlet of the existing stream during
the digging to keep any of the mud from invading the water
flow.

Dan Walker addressed Craig. "I understand you're going
to do the site construction?"

"That's right."

"Do you anticipate any problem with sending loose matter down the creek?"

The corner of Craig's mouth twitched, but his voice was
even and easy. "None. I'll use the hay, since it's in the
regulations. But as I'm sure you know, Mr. Walker, that
creek is so clogged up with silt and debris, the only way
anything would move down it is if it were carried by hand."

Dan Walker looked at him soberly for a second before
a grin split his face. He had been testing Craig, and Craig
knew it. Craig returned the grin. Letty sighed. Everyone
seemed to take to him. A woman-desired man's man. What
a phenomenon.

Dr. Fish's report took a full hour and a half. By the time
he finished, the group had been apprised of more facts and
figures than Letty had ever heard at one of these meetings.

When the doctor stopped talking, he stood still, his
expression a mixture of anticipation and anxiety. She realized the Prindles must have paid him a bundle to do all
that work and he was probably scared to death he might be
turned down.

Jess flipped through the report again, then shook his
head. "Until now, I always figured I was perfectly capable
of sitting on this board. But if I have to understand all the
stuff you just told us, Dr. Fish, I should resign tonight."
He sat back in his chair, arms crossed in front of him.

Dan assured Jess that he was not required to follow every
last detail. He then glanced through the official application
and turned to Craig. "Are you going to feed any of the water
directly into the pond?"

"No. In fact I'll be guarding against the intrusion of
ground water by humping the edges—not enough to look

artificial, but enough to contain the spring height as well as the fall."

Dan nodded, his confidence in Craig clear. "Anyone object to approving this?" No one did, so Dan put his signature on the page. "All set. Nice job, Dr. Fish. We learned a lot, even if we didn't have to."

Dr. Fish exhaled in clear relief. Craig looked over at Letty and winked, a simple gesture that caused a severe cramp in her resolution to emotionally dismiss him.

Getting out of the way of the couple that was presenting the next appeal, they walked out side by side, having been waved on by Dr. Fish, who was still collecting his charts. Craig held the heavy outside door for Letty. The foyer was too close a fit for her to avoid physical contact, and her arm brushed the front of his jacket. Despite her intention to avoid looking into those inviting depths, her eyes moved to his.

Craig didn't smile or say anything, yet the contact had the charge of a sharp shock of static electricity. And there was no question in her mind that this time the response was mutual.

She tripped on the doorsill, and his hand moved to steady her, then stayed in place as they headed for the parking lot. She'd have to practice falling over more often. It could be very effective. Neither of them spoke until they reached Letty's car. Then Craig asked, "Have you had dinner?"

"What a strange question. It's almost ten o'clock. Anyone in her right mind would have eaten by now." She smiled up at him, looking right into the magnetic fields through which he saw. "However, the answer is no, I haven't had dinner."

"Neither have I. Want to get a sandwich or an omelet or something?"

Oh yes, she most certainly wanted something. "What happened to the 'just a working relationship' bit?"

The gleam in his eyes could only be described as devilish. "I often eat with my fellow workers."

She looked at him for a minute, fighting her better instincts. "Listen, if an omelet sounds good to you, why don't we go to my house? Throwing together a few eggs is easy, and we'd have to drive a ways to find a restaurant open at this hour."

He didn't hesitate. "That sounds fine. I'll follow you."

She watched for just an instant as he headed toward his pickup; then she climbed behind her steering wheel. As she turned the key in the ignition, she tried to counsel herself about not taking chances, playing it safe, letting sleeping tigers lie, and... what was that other one? Oh yes, she reminded herself, little girls who play with fire...

She backed out of the parking lot, humming a tune about a lady who got so hot she burned down a whole town.

Letty was keenly aware of the high-set headlights following her out of the parking lot, through the center of town, around the two right turns, and down the winding street to her dark driveway. She felt truly alive, her heart pumping at increased tempo, her reflexes quick.

All the way home her mind was roiling, giving her endless instructions, bugging her about duty, honor, and truth in relationships. She was shocked to realize that her hands were shaking on the steering wheel as she made the turn around the circular drive into her garage. They were about to be alone in her house.

Well, almost alone. She smiled as she pictured Pudge in his waiting station on the other side of the door. But Pudge was not going to guard her from herself. She wanted this man—wanted him in her bed, in her body. The sleeping tigers had awakened, and they threatened to consume her.

Where's your willpower, Letty? she quizzed. She didn't know. It had been so long since she'd needed it she wasn't sure it still functioned.

She got out of the car, slamming the door behind her, wishing the bang would jolt her sense back to "good." It had no such effect. She activated the garage door and hastened out before it descended. They could have gone into the house through the garage, but she wanted to buy a little more unconfined time. That didn't help, either. Her traitorous conscience was still missing and showed no sign of returning to duty.

Craig was standing by the front door, his presence invading the dark night like a lighthouse. She fumbled for the key and shoved it into the lock.

"Hadn't you better deactivate the burglar alarm first?"

"Oh!" She started, embarrassed by her uncharacteristic ineptitude. "You're right. We were about to be joined by several members of the police force."

"You don't need *that* much protection from me."

She dropped her keys. A lot you know, she thought as he bent to retrieve them. She managed to turn off the alarm and open the door, aware that her sense of achievement at accomplishing same was way out of proportion. She reached in to turn on the light in the entrance hall.

"You should keep some lights on when you go out at night. It's pitch black out here. What good does a burglar alarm do when you have to fumble your way through the darkness to get to the front door?"

"Usually I come into the house through the garage."

"Oh." As they entered he bent to pet the purring cat, who had stepped forward immediately to greet him.

Letty looked down at the top of Craig's head. They had exhausted the subject of getting from a car into the house. What now? She wanted to reach out, to touch that thick, brown, silky-looking hair. She hung up her jacket in the coat closet and neatly placed her purse on the shelf. If a purse could look surprised, that one would have; it usually got tossed on a chair. But Letty needed something to do with her hands.

She walked into the other room with an overly jaunty step. "Do you want tea or coffee with your omelet, or something cold?"

Craig stood and followed her. "Tea would be nice. What can I do to help?"

I bet you know darn well what you could do to help. She opened the low cupboard, managing to knock a small stack of pans out onto the floor. "Damn." She glanced up, attempting a smile. "Sorry. Don't tell your dog I said that."

"My lips are sealed." They weren't sealed at all. They were slightly open in a gently curved smile. They were firm yet soft and oh so inviting.

"Thanks. I hate to shock animals." Her gaze swung to meet the bright, round, knowing eyes of her own animal. She felt like swearing again, this time at Pudge. He didn't have to look so all-fired smug! And the way he was sitting right next to Craig's foot, as though placing his stamp of approval on the man! She tried to zap Pudge with angry brain waves. After all, she was having enough trouble without his undisguised encouragement. "Pudge!" Her edginess showed in the pitch of her voice. "Don't get so close to Craig. You'll cover him with hair!"

In one fluid motion Craig scooped up the compliant cat. "Letty, I don't mind a few cat hairs. You seem nervous. Is anything wrong? I thought the conservation hearing went well."

She stood, frying pan in hand, and looked at him, searching for hidden messages. He was more inscrutable than the feline in his arms. "The meeting did go smoothly. I'm just a bit hyper lately. I don't know why." *Liar!* her mind shrieked. "My father tells me I work too hard. Maybe he's right."

She set about gathering eggs, green peppers, scallions, tomatoes, and cheddar cheese for a western omelet. It was her father's favorite, and she had a feeling Craig would like it, too. There was something about Craig that reminded her of her father, some quiet strength.

She soon realized it was disconcerting to try to work effectively with two pairs of gorgeous blue eyes following her every move. Immediately thereafter she dropped an egg on the floor. It smashed and oozed out on the linoleum. "Oh . . ."

"I'll clean it up." Craig set Pudge down and went past her to the roll of paper towels. With smooth efficiency he removed the gloppy mess from the floor. "Let me chop the vegetables. I'm worried about your fingers."

I'm a lot more worried about other parts of my body, she thought. With renewed determination, she accomplished the feat of breaking five eggs into a bowl, stirring them with a whisk, and adding a little milk. She put some small sausages on to braise and took out a loaf of the heavy brown bread she'd bought at the bakery in the next town. When she pulled out the sharp, serrated bread knife to slice it, Craig reached over and took it out of her hand. "The vegetables are ready," he said.

"I can certainly slice—" She stopped, noticing the telltale tremor in her fingers. She was losing patience with this show of schoolgirl twittery. "For crying out loud," she muttered, "I'm acting like a sixteen-year-old."

"Yeah, you are." When he grinned at her, it did nothing to relieve the symptoms. "It's very appealing."

"Maybe to you. It's giving *me* a pain in the neck."

"Would you like me to massage it for you?"

"Now look!" Damn, she'd almost stamped her foot again. "I don't know why you have this effect on me, but you do, and you obviously know you do. Inviting you over here was a mistake, but we *are* going to be working together, and I *should* be past this juvenile type of response. As you reminded me, I am engaged, and we are responsible adults! Now, let's get this omelet on the road!" She slapped the counter with a grand show of resolution.

"Omelets can't drive." Without any further acknowledgment of her declaration, he quietly continued to slice bread.

Letty stared at him, fighting concurrent urges to kick him, dump the eggs over his head instead of putting them in the pan, and interjecting her body between him and the butcher block and sliding her arms around his neck. "How can you calmly slice bread at a time like this?"

"You're engaged, right?"

"Right."

"Then I'd better slice bread."

"Craig!"

He turned and, with his maddening control intact, picked up the slices and placed them in her hand. When his fingers brushed hers she almost dropped the bread. "Letty, if the reaction you're having is even close to what's happening to me, then we're both fighting the inevitable, swimming upstream with the salmon."

His strong, hard hands cupped her face, tilting it toward his. Her lips parted in anticipation, but he didn't kiss her. He just held her, a captive of her wanting. "Challenging the current can be exciting for a while, but it'll wear both of us down eventually."

She closed her eyes for a moment, striving to quiet the clamor inside her, then opened them to confront him. "You're right, I know, but this has all happened so recently. How do I know . . ."

"Know what? That anything would work out with us? You don't. That's called 'taking a chance.' One thing, though, you *should* know."

She could scarcely breathe. "What?"

"You'd be nuts to marry Duane."

She jerked back from him. "Well, that's a fine thing to say! What makes you think that?"

"I only met him once, but it was clear you'd make mincemeat out of that guy in two weeks. And two weeks is giving him the benefit of the doubt."

She grabbed the frying pan, slapped it onto the burner, and turned up the heat. "Duane is a very nice man. He's sensitive and bright and good company."

"I didn't say he wasn't."

Her knife bit off a hunk of butter, which she slammed into the smoking pan. She quickly pushed the skillet off the burner to let it cool down. "I don't think this has anything to do with Duane. You and I don't even *know* each other, for pete's sake! What we're dealing with is simple chemistry!"

"You must be awfully smart. I never found anything about chemistry simple."

"You're deliberately clouding the issue!" She scraped the pan back onto the electric coil and flung in the onions and the green pepper, stirring them with a vengeance. "Just because I happen to meet someone who makes me a little hot under the collar . . ."

"Hot where?"

"Dammit!" She stamped her foot, then glared down at it. The dumb undisciplined thing!

"Letty . . ." Craig gently pushed her away from the stove and took over chef duties as his mellifluous voice, in an infuriatingly reasonable tone, asked, "What are you getting so mad about?"

Letty slumped onto a tall stool at the end of the countertop extension. "I don't know." She swiveled to face him squarely. "Yes I do. I don't usually bump into doorjambs and drop things, and I certainly don't run around falling all over strange men. Something peculiar has taken hold of me, and I feel silly and asinine."

He poured the eggs into the skillet. Did he need something to do with his hands, too? The thought was comforting.

"If it will make you feel any better, I'm not a very strange man. I'm quite normal and rather nice, all in all. And you don't need to feel silly. The chemistry, simple or not, is real—and mutual. I knew that when you first sat beside me at the Prindles'."

"Did you really?"

"Yes." He took the pan off the heat and divided the omelet between the two plates she had put on the counter. "Do you know what is the *last* thing I'm looking for at this particular point in my life?"

"No."

"You."

They completed the rest of the preparations in silence, then sat across from each other at the small oval table that sat by an open-hearth fireplace in a corner of the country kitchen. Pudge jumped up onto the upholstered side chair and curled himself into a ball. "Look at him." Letty was grappling for a conversational norm. "He acts like the most ordinary cat when he wants to eavesdrop."

Craig's eyes flicked from her to Pudge to his plate. "Very effective. I'd take him for a cat any day." He spread some of her homemade jam on his toast. "Mmm, delicious. Western omelets are my favorite."

"I had a feeling they might be."

"Oh? Why is that?"

"My dad likes them."

"There's a message there."

"Yes."

They finished the late supper in a continuation of the earlier wary silence, eyes meeting briefly, then lowering. Letty tried to relax her taut neck muscles. She had been giving herself a literal pain in the neck, and yes, thank you, she *would* like him to massage it.

But why *did* she get so mad? She was aware he was giving them both defusing time, and she tried to be grateful for it. But she had to admit, way back in the secret, most honest part of her brain, that she'd have been far more grateful if that control of his had snapped and he had torn her clothes off and taken her in the middle of the living room rug.

She took a big gulp of her tea, feeling the warm liquid slide all the way down her throat and settle in her stomach, where it sent out comforting heat vapors. Was there a part of her that wanted to be dominated? If so, she had fought it with spitfire ferocity for as many years as she could remember.

One person she'd never steamrolled, however, was her father. Caleb had never severely punished her; it hadn't been necessary. There had simply been a look that came into his eyes that stopped her cold, sending a powerful though silent message: "Halt!" She had already sighted a like message in Craig's eyes on several occasions.

"What are you thinking about?"

She looked up. "My father."

"The two of you seem to be good friends."

"Yes. I was just remembering my childhood years, when I sometimes thought of him as the enemy. I can't quite recall when that changed."

"I'll bet you were a feisty kid."

She laughed. "I plead guilty. I'm sure I account for a lot of the gray in Dad's hair. She grinned at Craig. "But I've become docile. Maybe that's why we can be friends now."

"Uh-huh. Tell me another." He set his mug on the table. "I never had much time for trouble when I was growing up. Too busy working."

"Are your parents both living?"

"Yes, thank God. We have a close family. We all live in New Hampshire. I have two other brothers besides the one who works with me. All three are married and have kids. Holidays in our family are pretty crazy."

"I'll bet they're fun."

"Yeah, they are." He ate a piece of toast, watching her in a speculative way. "Letty, what was your husband like?"

Her fork slipped from her grasp and fell to the floor. Pudge jumped from his chair and went over to sniff at it. Unimpressed, he returned to the warmed seat. Letty leaned over slowly to retrieve the utensil.

"Did I bring up a bad subject?"

She shook her head while she refilled her teacup, put in a spoonful of sugar, and stirred. "No, not really. It was hard for me to discuss John for a long time, but that's over, finally."

"You must have loved him a great deal for the pain of losing him to last this long."

Her eyes lifted to his. "Craig...remember when you told me about the woman you almost married, the one who walked out on you?"

"Yes."

"You said you were over the hurt, but it was the anger that remained."

"Yes."

"I've never been sure how much of which I was dealing with. I loved him, then hated him, then...I don't know."

"Do you mind talking about it?"

"Not really." She nervously nibbled the edge of a piece of toast. "John was the son of some of my parents' friends, so it seemed as if I always knew him. He grew up to be handsome and witty and popular with the girls. I had such a crush on him all through junior high and high school and college. The year I was finishing my master's degree was when he finally seemed to notice me."

"Did he have a problem with his eyesight?"

She smiled at him gratefully. "Thank you, that's nice. I've never had any illusions about my looks."

Craig looked genuinely surprised. "I don't know what you mean. You're a very pretty woman."

She was right. He was a gentleman. "Thank you again. Anyway, John was always otherwise occupied, by one girl after another. Isn't it amazing? He never stuck to anyone for long, yet when he proposed I assumed he would automatically settle down. And I was so proud he'd chosen me!"

"And?"

"We had a spectacular start. He was the vice-president of his father's office-machines business and made lots of money for such a young man. I think his father kept assuming he'd settle down, too. Anyway, we bought a house right away and joined the country club, where we played golf and tennis and went to the dances. I jumped into landscaping with great enthusiasm—he never minded that I was sometimes late getting home and all . . ."

"Sounds pretty ideal."

"Yeah, great. We had three terrific years—lots of fun, lots of friends. Then I found out *why* he didn't mind my being busy."

"Uh-oh."

"You can say that again. I won't go into detail; I'm sure you get the picture. Anyway, I forgave him, after he swore it would never happen again. And we had a couple more pretty good years. I thought he'd kept his promise. Until one cold, icy night when his car slid off the road and into a tree."

"So that's how it happened."

"Yes. I was devastated. I thought nothing could cause

more pain than that. I was wrong. It got lots worse when I found out that one of my 'close friends' was with him."

"Ah, Letty, you must have been so hurt."

"Hurt, mad, astounded, disillusioned—you name it."

"You're sure it wasn't just . . ."

"I'm sure. I went to see her that night in the hospital. She blurted it all out, told me how sorry she was—kind of a confessional. She probably wouldn't have done it if she'd known she was going to be all right."

Craig didn't say anything for a minute; then he softly asked, "So . . . enter Duane?"

"Over quite a long period, yes. He's been kind and thoughtful. A nice companion."

"Sounds like a good person to spend your later years with . . . say from about eighty-five on."

"Oh? And what's so great about passion, anyway? John provided plenty of that. Why not? He had all that experience." She stared at the last bite of egg coagulating on the plate. "And what about you? You probably had rockets and flares and all that with the woman who didn't marry you. What good did it do you?"

"It made me feel alive, while it lasted."

"I feel alive when I plant a row of marigolds. I get nearly ecstatic over a particularly choice mountain laurel. And not one of them has ever broken my heart."

Craig rose and walked around the table to stand by her chair. He put out a hand, and by reflex she took it and stood beside him. He took her other hand and held them, warming them in his sturdy grasp.

"Letitia. Getting hurt isn't the end of the world. Once you stop exposing yourself to that possibility, you're packing up a lot of the best part of being human. You shouldn't try to cancel out your emotions." His smoky glance caressed her. "Can you honestly say you don't feel anything stirring right now?"

Her head moved back and forth. "No."

"I think you're lovely, and I admire your gutsiness and

your knowledge and your independence. And I do believe that you and I together just might make one hell of a good team."

She raised her eyes to his, captivated by his sincerity and by the unrelenting power of his physical draw. "I hate to admit this, after you've said all those nice things, but I'm scared of my emotions."

"I can't fault you for that. But I'll repeat what I said earlier: We're in it already. It's just a matter of time." He dropped her hands and turned to scratch Pudge's head in farewell. "I even like your cat."

Letty couldn't believe he was actually going. She followed him into the entryway. "You're leaving?"

"Yes."

"But . . ."

He turned abruptly and grasped her shoulders tightly. There was a pause, only seconds long, during which her heart refused to beat. She needed his kiss so desperately, and he had walked away from it before.

His mouth took hold of hers with sovereign authority, two lips that knew their predestined goal. They moved with a need close to harshness, his body closing the gap to cling to hers.

The taste of him raged through her, and her earth moved. Much too quickly, he let her go. "You're not the only one who's scared." He opened the door. "Better get some rest. We have a war coming up over a pond. That may be enough for now." He turned and left.

Letty absolutely *never* went to bed without cleaning up the kitchen, but she went to bed without cleaning up the kitchen. She lay awake for a long time, stroking Pudge's soft fur, going over every word said, every gesture made, every look exchanged, trying, without success, to make some sense of it.

She had a very erotic dream that night. It did not involve Duane.

- 5 -

WHEN LETTY AWOKE the next morning she felt dazed and disoriented. She swung her legs over the side of the bed and sat up, glancing at the clock. Five forty-five. What day was today? Oh yes, Thursday. She wasn't expected anywhere until nine. She could have a real breakfast and a second cup of coffee. What luxury! Then she remembered the unwashed dishes and groaned.

She moved mechanically through the routine of showering, dressing, and making the bed, puzzled at the gnawing churlishness that had such a firm grip on her mood. She kept thinking about the night before, trying to dismiss the disruptive sensations that had invaded her system.

Looking out her bedroom window, she could see it was going to be a glorious day. The sun was creeping over the horizon, lighting the immaculately clear sky. Where was the usual leap of delight that came with opening the doors and windows to the quickly warming air?

One thing that had not vanished since the night before

was the affliction of clumsiness. During the brief period it took to clean up the kitchen, she dropped two forks, one knife, the loaf of bread, and a cup, which bounced off an open drawer she'd forgotten to close and crashed to the floor in tiny pieces.

"Dammit!" she screamed at the top of her lungs, glad at least to be alone and free to vent her frustration. She snatched the dustpan and whisk broom out of the closet, hitting her finger in the process. "Dammit!" she shrieked again, even louder.

"Letty?" She heard the bang of the front screen door as her father's voice preceded him into the room. "Whatever's the matter?"

She looked up from the floor, stopping the furious action of the whisk broom that had sent some of the broken pieces into the dustpan and some flying over the side and back onto the floor. "Hi, Dad."

"Hi, Dad? That's it? That's an awfully normal greeting for someone who was yelling blue murder when I came in."

She swept up the remaining shards and dumped them into the trash can. "It was only a broken cup. I just woke up on the wrong side of my disposition."

"Uh-oh. Maybe I'd best retreat and come back later."

"No, stay. I'd like your company. There's a pot of coffee almost brewed, and I'll whip up some pancakes." Her eyes moved anxiously to him. "You haven't eaten yet, have you?"

"No, I ran over to catch you before you left. I discovered I hadn't returned those nursery catalogues, and I noticed you had them all marked up, so I thought you might need them for ordering." He took two mugs out of the cupboard, filled them with coffee, and handed one to Letty, who had set about the job of mixing the pancake batter. "What accounts for your bad humor? Last night was the conservation meeting, wasn't it? Did something go wrong?"

She whipped the batter to a smooth blend and checked to see if the frying pan was heating. "The meeting went smoothly. Swimmingly, in fact." She recounted the story of Dr. Fish and was rewarded by her father's amusement.

"Okay." Caleb set placemats and silverware on the table and filled two glasses with orange juice. "So why the dour expression?"

Letty took her time answering. She poured batter for three pancakes into the pan, satisfied by the sizzle as it touched the surface. "Dad, Craig came back here after the meeting. Neither of us had eaten, so I made us an omelet and . . ." She shrugged helplessly. "I don't know. He's got me all confused."

Caleb sat down on the stool and studied her face. "Sounds like the 'business relationship' has turned into something else."

She barely glanced at him as she flipped the pancakes. "Well, not really. Let's just say it has that potential."

"Yes. Let's say that."

This time she did look at him. "Are you teasing me?"

Caleb stood up. "Whoops! We forgot the syrup." He went to the refrigerator, took out the tin of Vermont maple syrup, and poured some into a small pan to heat. "No, Letty, I'm not teasing. When I met Craig Sullivan I had one of my instant premonitions you're always so skeptical about. I thought to myself, 'Now here's a man who's a match for my daughter.' Looks like the same thing has occurred to you."

The second batch of flapjacks were ready to be turned, and Letty was glad to have this chore between her and direct contact with her father. It was always such a comfort to talk to him, but there were certain things a woman just couldn't share with her father. Yet her need for consultation forced her to sift through the list of permissible topics.

"It has occurred to me. But, Dad," she protested as she slid the pancakes onto a platter, poured the syrup into a pitcher, carried both to the table, and sat down facing her father. "It also occurs to me that I'm taking this awfully seriously, and it's probably just one of those crazy physical attractions that should be chuckled about and then forgotten."

"Letitia, my girl," Caleb began, heaping his plate with

steaming hotcakes and passing the platter to her, "you are not old enough to refer to physical attraction as a silly thing to be chuckled over. You need a little passion in your life."

"I have—"

"Please! Don't say you have Duane. I want to enjoy my meal."

"You're too tough on Duane, Dad. In most ways he's just what I need. How could I fit someone who demanded a lot of time into my schedule? As for Craig, when I woke up this morning, I realized that I met him just over one month ago and have only *seen* him three times. And it's obvious he's almost as skittish about this attraction as I am. Maybe I should do what Duane suggested—marry him right after the Prindle job. It *is* about time I set a date."

"Letty . . ." His tone commanded her full attention. "You'd be nuts to marry Duane."

She lowered her head into her hands, shaking it back and forth. "Good gravy, it's mental telepathy! As if I haven't enough to contend with without that!" She looked up at him with her first smile of the morning. "Craig said exactly the same thing."

"See? I was right; he is smart—thinks like me."

"Deliver me! Well, the two of you can get together and have smugness contests if you like. But I'm going to stick to what I think is best for me. I've been very content the last couple of years, and I'm willing to settle for that. By this time next year Mr. Sullivan will be but a dim memory." With an unconvincing show of resolution, she started to carry the dishes to the sink.

Caleb stood, his motion weighted with a trace of weariness. "You always were bullheaded, Letty. Born under the wrong star. Dreadful combination: red hair and a Taurus."

She turned to smile at what she assumed was a humorous remark, but Caleb's expression was dead serious. "Dad? Don't worry about me. I'll be all right."

"I do worry about you. It's hard for a parent to watch a child make an obvious mistake."

"I'm not a child, Dad."

"Sometimes you are. Sometimes we all are. The capacity for being childlike is good. But being childish isn't."

She stopped her activity and regarded him in puzzlement. It had been a long time since he'd given her a lecture, but this sounded very much like the beginning of one. "I should think the childish thing in this case would be to dissolve a relationship I feel comfortable with and jump into one that might be completely wrong for me. I don't *want* to be shaken up, Dad. I want my life to be orderly and foreseeable and calm."

"Letitia Aldridge, there is nothing in your biological or emotional makeup that has fitted you for a life that is incessantly orderly and foreseeable and calm. You're trying to turn yourself into something you're not, and that isn't a good idea for anyone. I know it's hard sometimes not to rebel against a parent's advice, at any age. But if you'd look back far enough, you might remember that I also told you you'd be nuts to marry John Aldridge."

"Dad . . ."

"I know, I've never thrown that one up at you, but maybe it's time I did. Now"—he kissed her on the cheek—"I am going to play golf. And I'm going to play golf with a lovely lady of fifty-plus years who makes my aged heart go pitter-patter. So, while you slip away into tedium, I am going to kick up my heart rate." He gave her a wave and headed for the door, having to stop, of course, to pat Pudge, who had finally gotten out of bed.

Letty stared after him in shocked muteness. She *had* forgotten his warning about John. At the time it was given, she'd been completely unwilling to entertain doubts about her dream man. Dream man, huh! No wonder Duane seemed like a good alternative to that kind of entanglement.

Speaking of entanglements . . . why hadn't she heard about this lady her father was seeing? Caleb hadn't shown any undue interest in a woman in years. And just what was undue? He was more than entitled to any happiness he could grab. Heaven knew life was short enough!

She stared down at the round blue eyes that were staring

up at her. "And what about me, Pudge? Do I grab, too?"

She prepared his cat food and set it on the floor, then squatted beside him as he ate. "I have a confession to make. I'm scared to death of Craig Sullivan. I think Dad's right; he *is* a match for me—and I've become used to having my own way."

Ready to begin her day's rounds, she stood, but she continued her conversation with Pudge. "The one thing I've always been able to count on is my work. I'm good at it, and I have control over the results. Neither of those factors applies once you let your heart get too involved." She leaned over to give Pudge a last pat. "It's far better to play it safe."

Pudge just kept eating, apparently seeing nothing in that statement worth reacting to.

Letty gathered up her clipboard and sketches and calendar and nursery catalogues. She had an appointment at nine with a prospective client for a job the following spring. After that she planned to go to three nurseries to select some of the plants for her current jobs. She was particularly anxious to get to Wesbank's to look at a weeping hemlock that was supposed to be particularly choice.

Just as she was about to walk out the door the phone rang. Her heart skipped a beat. She hesitated. Should she answer? What if . . . ? Exasperated at her shilly-shallying, she strode into the den and picked up the phone. "Hello?"

"Mrs. Aldridge?"

"Yes."

"This is Jerry Lawrence in Weston. I'm having some work done by a Mr. Craig Sullivan. He's repairing a dam for me."

"Oh, then he *did* take that job."

"Yes. He recommended you for some landscaping we have in mind. I understand you're very busy, but this wouldn't have to be done right away. It could be done this fall or even next spring if necessary."

"That sounds good. Would you like me to come see what you have in mind?"

He sounded relieved. "Yes, by all means. Whenever

you're able to come, my wife and I will arrange to be here."

After checking her calendar, Letty made arrangements to see them in two weeks. Craig Sullivan was not making it easy for her to stop thinking about him.

Before she could make it out the door, the phone rang again. "Damn. I'm never going to get out of here!" She grabbed the receiver with one hand while juggling all her materials in the other. "Yes?"

"Letty, I'm glad I caught you."

"Oh, Jim, hi. What's up?"

"Roger Jenkins called. He can bring the backhoe to the Prindles' this morning. There's been a hitch in his other job." Letty hired Roger for all of her jobs that required the use of a backhoe.

"What did you tell him?"

"I took a chance and said yes. You know what'll probably happen otherwise; he'll still be on the other job when he *is* due at the Prindles."

"You're right, and we don't have any spare time to get those big plants out of the way before the major digging starts. And no way could we get them out with shovels! I'll call and cancel this morning's appointment, then meet you there. You know most of what we want moved anyway."

"Okay. When is the Sullivan equipment due to be brought in?"

"Next Wednesday morning."

"Whew. We've got a little work to do between now and then."

"You'd better believe it. See you at the Prindles'."

"Right."

Letty made a call to reschedule her nine o'clock meeting with the new prospective clients, then put the receiver back in the cradle. With a sigh, she headed upstairs to change into her grub clothes. It was bound to be another mud-pie day.

Letty had been right about the mud. By the time she got home that night she was covered with it. They'd had an awful time getting at some of the small trees and large plants she wanted rescued from alongside the stream. The backhoe had come dangerously close to getting stuck several times, and it had become clear, early on, that anything around the pond site that was too large to dig by hand would have to be rescued by Craig's machine, since it was able to work on soft ground.

But through the chaos of the day, the germ of an idea had begun to grow. She had a wonderful plan for the area behind where the pond would be, and she'd made arrangements to sit down with the Prindles over breakfast the next morning to discuss it with them. Her exhaustion was forgotten once she was clean and fed and had her sketching pad on the table in front of her. This was going to be beautiful. She could see it now.

From the moment she opened her eyes, the following morning seemed brighter and more promising than its predecessor. She hummed while she made coffee and gave Pudge a can of his favorite cat food. "The Prindles are going to *love* this idea, Pudge. It's brilliant, a stroke of true inspiration."

Within an hour she found out that the Prindles did love it. They reflected, and intensified, her own enthusiasm. Ellen, who was particularly vocal about the project, sat next to Letty at the breakfast table on the terrace. Since the pool was just two steps down and twenty feet away, Letty had a chance to view the pond site from what was apparently one of Ellen's favorite vantage points.

"Oh, it's going to be wonderful!" Ellen gushed. "Just think, lovey"—she reached over to tap her husband's arm—"if we have some little Prindles one of these days, we could make a miniature ski run for them!"

Letty cleared her throat. "It would be *quite* miniature. And I'm not sure you'd want to have children shooting down a ski run across a pond."

Ellen giggled. "We *would* have to be sure the ice was thick enough, wouldn't we? Unless, of course"—she giggled again—"it happened to be Bart's darling little boy from his last marriage."

Bart Prindle looked annoyed. "I'm afraid your humor has a macabre twist now and again, Ellen."

"Who's joking?" She arched her eyebrows at him in a gesture that, to Letty, seemed to be poised on the fine line between teasing and taunting.

"I think I'll leave ski slopes to someone else," Letty concluded lightly, gathering up her sketches and pushing back her chair. "I must get to work. There are still lots of frightened plants out there waiting to be rescued from the mad heavy-construction diggers." She didn't want to get involved in an altercation between the Prindles, especially since each time she saw Ellen she liked her better. There was much more that was right up front about the woman than her impressive bosom.

Bart Prindle stood. "You'll have to review your plans with Craig, of course. He's due to stop by here late this afternoon, so you can check with him then."

Check with him, can I? she inwardly fumed. I'll *tell* him! "Fine. Don't let him get away without seeing me," she responded brightly.

"We won't." Bart shook her hand before sitting down to pour himself another cup of coffee.

Ellen walked down to the bottom step of the terrace with Letty. "That Craig Sullivan is just about the cutest thing I've ever seen," she confessed in a low tone. "He could certainly tempt me right off the straight and narrow. Unfortunately, I get the feeling he's very straight himself, although he's certainly not narrow." She grinned at Letty. "Why don't *you* take a shot at him? Perhaps, incredible as the thought may be, he's more receptive to women who are available in a more permanent sense."

Letty returned the grin. "Well now, Ellen, I just might do that—take a shot, that is."

"Good luck to you, honey. Not that I promise to drop out of the race, mind you. Of course so far I don't even feel like a contender." She stopped at the bottom of the steps and gazed down at Jim and Len, who had already started digging at the edge of the creek off to the left. "All that rippling muscle! It sure improves the scenery around here." She turned her attention back to Letty. "Listen, have breakfast with us whenever you can. We usually eat out here when the weather's good."

Letty was pleased to see that the invitation was extended with a smile of genuine friendliness. "I'll take you up on that," she replied. "It was a real treat. Have a nice day!" With a cheerful wave, she went to plunge into the day's labor.

Letty crawled up the steep banking, struggling to keep her balance while she juggled a large clump of marsh marigolds in her right hand. When she got to the top she sank to the ground to rest.

Len came over and sat beside her. "Boy, will I be glad when this part of the job is done," he confessed, running a grimy hand along his pant leg.

Letty watched the gesture and laughed. "That won't do you any good. You can't clean your hand on your pants when your pants are dirtier than your hand!"

"Thanks for the profound observation." He shook his head. "Why do we have to do all this rescue work? The Prindles can sure as hell afford to buy new plants. And you know these won't all make it; wild vegetation hates to be transplanted. Come to think of it, that's probably why it's called wild." He grinned at her. "There you go, one profound statement in exchange for another."

"Now, Len, you're just tired. It'd be a crime to let all these lovely things get wiped out. And most of them will make it. Besides, we'd never find new ones this large."

"So let 'em grow. For a creek that's supposed to be almost filled in, this one has a lot of water and very steep sides."

"Only in places, Len. Be fair. It's completely clogged in a few sections, enough to stalemate the flow."

"Tell me about it. I smell like a septic tank." He stood and looked toward the house. "Someone's waving. Is that intended for you, or should I just wave back?"

Letty stood, too, to get a better view. "Oh. That's Craig Sullivan. I have to talk to him. Do you want to come up and meet him?"

"Naw. I'll wait until next week. In my present condition, I might bowl him over with my eau de swamp."

She laughed. "I think he's hardier than that. What time is it?"

"Four-fifteen."

"Why don't you and the others knock it off. We've put in a full day, and there's no way we can finish this now. It'll take at least one more working day, maybe more."

"Okay, Letty. I'm ready to go home. See you Monday."

"Bye-bye."

When she started the hike up to the house, she became aware of her own weariness. As she got closer and was able to see Craig more clearly, she also became aware of her mud-streaked condition. Maybe she could talk him into coming back to the house for a drink so she could take a quick shower before their discussion. But as she climbed the terrace steps, she saw that he was almost as dirty as she was.

"Hi, Craig. Been playing in the mud?"

"That's about it. Looks like you have been, too. We should have played together."

The laughing eyes teased her with the proposition. Even rolling around in a swamp with him sounded appealing. "As a matter of fact, that's what I wanted to talk to you about."

"Playing in the mud together?"

"Well, close. *Digging* in the mud is more like it."

"Ah. We're back to ponds and creeks."

"Yes. I have some sketches to show you, but they're out in the car. Do you want to wait here while I get them, or should we go back to my place?"

"Can we play in the mud if we do?"

"No, we cannot. I simply thought that before we talked I might be able to slip into something comfortable, like a shower."

"Playing in the shower sounds even better."

"Craig . . . remember my 'spoken for' status."

"That's right. In that case, we might as well stay put. Ellen's bringing me a glass of lemonade, so I'll wait out here while you get the papers."

She stared at him. He was back to inscrutable. So Ellen was bringing him a glass of lemonade. Letty hoped it was sour. "I'll be right back."

"I'll be waiting."

She tried not to rush, but the mental image of Ellen Prindle leaning over to hand Craig a cold drink did nothing to cool Letty down. "It's none of your damned business," she snapped at herself. So what if Ellen's a gorgeous blonde? If Mr. oh-so-scrupulous Sullivan won't come near *you* because you're engaged, he darned well ought to stay away from *Mrs*. Prindle. The mental tirade went on for the entire journey to the car and back. And at this time of day and her stage of weariness, a journey it was.

When she got back to the terrace, Ellen was sitting next to Craig. Next to? She was practically sitting on top of him, or at least as close to that as was possible in a separate chair. Letty could hear the ominous rattle of her temper mechanism activating itself. She strove to shut it off as she approached the two people.

"Well, here she is." Ellen smiled up at her. "Pull up a seat, Letty. Will you have lemonade, or would you like something stronger?"

Letty forced a smile. Ellen was being so kind, it wouldn't be fair to kick her in the shins. Although it hardly seemed fair for her to sit there in her pristine blond beauty while Letty looked like an ad entitled *Feed This Homeless Refugee*. "Lemonade is fine, thank you."

The three of them chatted in a relaxed way for a few minutes until Ellen said, "I'll leave you two alone to discuss the hill. I've already seen the plans, and it'll be easier for you to figure out how it's to be done without me here." She stood and crossed behind Craig, then gave Letty a broad wink as she left. Letty could have kissed her.

When Ellen had disappeared into the house, Craig raised his eyebrows at Letty. "Hill?"

Letty unrolled the sketches. "Wait until you see. This is a marvelous stroke, if I do say so myself. And it'll relieve you of the time-consuming job of hauling away any of the dirt you dig out of either the creek or the pond!"

"So far I like it. What have you come up with? An air lift for dirt?"

"No. Something even better."

He pulled his chair next to hers by the table. "Ah. I see you have a kidney-shaped pond there. Good girl. But that shaded area behind it must be either a hill or a drop-off." He looked out over the scene before them, as though confirming his memory. "I was right; there's neither."

"Not now. That's absolutely true. But just envision how lovely it would be to *have* a slight hill right there. A rising slope would form a perfect backdrop. I thought you could dump whatever waste you dig, and we could bring in more dirt if needed for the right height."

"Letty, that's not a good place for a rise. I'll be trying to route the ground water away from the pond, not into it."

"But the slope would be well back from where the pond will be."

"You didn't check those water tables very thoroughly. All you'd need is one of Dr. Fish's ten-year-high rainstorms and your new hill would slide to the bottom of the pond."

"Craig, that is *so* unlikely to happen."

"Yes, it's unlikely. But I remember once, before I owned the crane, when Tony Bellini gave in to a property owner's request against the advice of the experts and dug a beautiful pond that would have held up against any but one of the hundred-year drenches."

"I feel an unwelcome message coming on, but go ahead."

"He had to redig it, at his own expense, after the flood waters receded."

"But that's not fair, if he was doing what the owner wanted. Who can predict a flood?"

"The owner developed a case of instant amnesia. He just waved the hydrology report in front of Tony's eyes and threatened to sue. People are like that, unfortunately. Besides, this is your idea, not the Prindles'."

"Not entirely; they love it."

"That's nice. But I won't dig it that way. And getting huge truckloads of dirt in there across that marshy ground would be mighty interesting. Even more interesting would be getting huge equipment in to pull them out."

"You make me sound like a ninny. Of course I know a big truck couldn't go in there, but you told me yourself how much material will come out of the ground between digging the pond and the creek, and a truck could drop the dirt here"—her finger jabbed at the plan—"and your backhoe could move it in."

"Even a backhoe would stand a good chance of sinking in that ground."

She had to admit, if only mentally, that he was right. "Well, the dirt has to be moved around after you dig it out. Surely you don't do that by hand!"

"No. We do it with a wide-bodied bulldozer. The kind I told you about that's built close to the ground for just that purpose; the weight is more evenly distributed so it can maneuver on soft earth."

"Then why can't you move extra dirt in with that? I should think you'd like the idea. It would be far easier to drop the pond waste right there than to haul it off somewhere. And I still don't believe a rise that slight would create a hazard. I'm not exactly a novice at this, you know."

"You're an expert in your field, which is landscape architecture, not hydrology or site development. I happen to be an engineer, and I tell you it's a bad place for an incline of any dimension. I won't put one in. I want that pond to be trouble free for about twenty years, at which point, at worst, the Prindles might have some cleaning out to do."

"But I—"

"Letty, no hills. For crying out loud, they have a private park back here as it is. They can live without a mountain of their own."

"They happen to *want* a hill, and they can *afford* a hill! We should build them a bloody monument, if that's what they want. It's their property!"

"Are you sure it's *their* monument you want to build?"

She straightened up, her face aflame with indignation. "Are you suggesting that I want to erect a monument to myself?"

"Most architects do."

"Why you . . . !" She grabbed the plans and rolled them up furiously. "How dare you? You have no reason to question my integrity!"

"I'm not questioning your integrity—just your judgment. And most architects—landscape or otherwise—*do* want to create visual testimonials to their craft. It's perfectly natural. The Prindles can afford just about anything, and they're giving you free rein. That's pretty heady stuff. I admit a hill would look good there, but that doesn't change the fact that it's a bad location for one. In fact, if there were already a hill there, I'd recommend flattening it."

Insulted and livid, Letty slapped the rolled paper against the table and started to rise. Craig clamped his hand on her arm and stopped her. "Letty"—his voice was very low—"helping a pseudo teenager make an omelet was a kick. Working with one on an important job would be anything but."

Her grip on the roll of paper tightened. She had an overwhelming urge to smash him over the head with it. Then her eyes met his. They were not angry, but they held a gentle warning. She felt her anger waver. "Why the devil do you have to win on everything?"

"What does it have to do with winning? This is a job, not a contest."

"I'm not trying to turn it into a contest! But I get something in my mind's eye that looks so beautiful, and then I get shot down by some"—she waved her hands in the air—"construction type!"

"We 'construction types' are like that. We feel better if we know what we build today will still be there the day after tomorrow. My father had continuous problems with architects all the years he was in the house-building business. It's a matter of priorities. Builders are primarily interested in a good structure at a fair cost."

"And just what do you think architects are interested in?"

"Monuments."

"Why you—you pigheaded mud-mover! I'm every bit as concerned about cost and reliable results as you are. You're just going to come in and dig a damn hole in the ground, then go riding off into the sunset on your bucking backhoe! I'll be working on this project long after you've come and gone." She forced her voice down a few decibels. It was so frustrating to fight with someone whose tone never rose above reasonable! "If something goes wrong, I'm the one who'll be right here to take the blame!"

"That sounds very logical, but it's not how it would work. If, five years from now, there was an exceptional storm and the Prindles' pond got half filled in, I can guarantee they'd come hammering at *my* door, demanding to know why I hadn't told them not to put a slope behind their pond. I can also guarantee they wouldn't recall that I had."

Letty jumped up and strode back and forth, fighting to get her professionalism back in tow. He *did* know a lot more about what they were talking about than she did. Why was it so hard for her to accept that gracefully? He was right; she did seem to be turning everything they discussed into a contest. It was time to stop it. "All right, all right. No hill. But we'd darn sure better have one whale of a storm in the next ten years, or I'm going to be ticked!"

"Mark it off on the calendar; you're entitled to one free tantrum if there's been no hurricane or at least a properly severe nor'easter by the end of a decade."

She whirled, ready to hurl a few more harsh words his

way, but the corners of his mouth had that upward tilt, and his dreamy, summer-sky eyes were twinkling. The combination pricked her ballooning anger, and the hot air of hostile words drained out. "Oh . . . nuts!"

His eyes widened, then crinkled with laughter. "Oh nuts? Is that the best you can do at the end of a perfectly good snit?"

She crossed the terrace and sank back into her chair. "Yes, it's the best I can do. I was tired when we started this, and it's truly exhausting to carry on an argument after it's been proven you're wrong."

He fell back in his chair. "Is this a day I should mark on *my* calendar? Am I mistaken, or is it perhaps a bit unusual for you to admit to being wrong?"

"It's damn unusual, so don't get used to it. You caught me at the end of a long, hard day."

He leaned forward, his chin on his fists, his face close to hers. "In that case, I'll endeavor to see that you're rested and fresh for our next combat."

"What? You hate victory?"

"Not at all. But you're awfully cute when you're mad."

This time she did whack him over the head with the roll of paper. "Just had to push your luck, didn't you!"

"That's not what I'd really like to push."

"Craig!" Letty was thrown entirely off balance by his on-again off-again tactics. She stood so quickly her chair toppled over. "Ohhh . . . !" Before she could turn to pick it up, Craig had risen and righted the chair.

"Letty . . ." He was visibly trying not to laugh. "Come on, I'll walk you to your car."

Ignoring the man at her side, she charged off in the direction of the driveway, but as she felt her blood pressure slowly settle back toward normal, she shortened her strides. "I'm sorry," she made herself say. "I *have* been behaving like a child. I don't understand it. I really thought I had my temper under better control at this point in my life."

"You do seem to be trying to live up to that red hair. But don't worry about it. I can take care of myself."

She stopped and looked at him squarely. "Yes, I'll just bet you can."

When they reached her car, he opened the door for her. "Letty..."

"What?"

"Why don't you break that damn engagement?"

She slid into the driver's seat, then looked up at him. "I've begun to ask myself the same question."

"I wish you'd get around to answering it." He cupped her chin with his hand and bent to her, his lips brushing hers with infuriating brevity. "We could make beautiful fireworks together."

Her voice came out in a croak. "Isn't that supposed to be *music?*"

He grinned. "I have a feeling any score we wrote would have to be performed by a ninety-piece percussion band." He touched her lips with his fingers. "I'll see you...probably here."

She nodded, still captivated by the lingering warmth on her lips. "That's right. Next Wednesday."

"Wednesday?"

"Yes. You're due to bring the equipment in on Wednesday and start the work on Thursday, right? Will you dig the pond or the creek first?"

He looked down at her, frowning slightly. "Well, I *hope* to get here next week. Actually, I'm digging the dam at the Lawrences', and it's causing a few extra headaches. We've had to do some reinforcing at one end before I can finish the digging. I may not be able to move the crane until late Friday afternoon or Monday morning, but I think the boys can bring over the Grade-all and start the creek by Thursday or Friday."

"Craig! I've built my whole schedule around being here when you come in."

"I told you not to do that, Letty. It takes a lot of time to get the machines moved, and I can't be absolutely sure how long a job will take. Besides, your involvement doesn't start until my part of it ends."

She stared up at him in disbelief. "We've been over this before. I want to be there when the digging is done."

"Then be there. But don't try to pin me to an exact hour, because I can't operate that way."

"You *should* be able to. You took the Prindle job before the Lawrence job. If you're running into problems with the Lawrences' dam, it hardly seems fair to postpone the Prindles' pond while you solve them."

The blue eyes were developing a steely-gray cast. "And just what do I do? Leave the Lawrences with a half-dug dam?"

"Can't you go back there after you finish here? I'm sure they'd understand if you explained that this was your first commitment."

"Would they understand the extra thousand-dollar expense of moving the crane from Weston to Sherborn and back to Weston again?"

"It seems to me your time could be a little better planned. I've structured my whole week around being here when you come in, and you should get yourself here next Wednesday!"

The gray in his eyes had obliterated the soft blue. "Letitia, just one word of caution about my disposition. It stays pretty even most of the time, but when I blow, I blow. Ask, but don't order. Orders, as we discussed once before, don't sit well with me."

Letty stared back at him, unblinking. "All right, no orders. Pretty please with sugar on it . . . get your ass here next Wednesday!"

"It will arrive here, seated on one of my machines, when I am damn good and ready to bring it."

She opened her mouth, then reconsidered and closed it. What had almost come out was, as her mother used to say, beyond the pale. She slammed the door shut and, tires squealing, tore out of the Prindle driveway, almost running down a flinty-eyed Irishman who no longer looked calm.

- 6 -

As it turned out, Letty and her men had more than enough time to remove the endangered plants from the Prindle creek. There was no sign of a single Sullivan machine on Wednesday. There was no sign of a single Sullivan machine on Thursday. By Friday at noon Letty was so mad she was afraid to speak to anyone for fear of what would escape her lips.

Her three men were concerned only with planting the thirty-seven shrubs that had been delivered by the Wesbank Nursery to the Fraziers' new house. Ordinarily Letty would have concentrated her energies on that job, too, and put the other out of her mind. But by lunchtime Friday she had driven to the Prindles' house twice to see if anything was happening.

"Letty, why are you getting so upset about this?" Jim sat beside her on one of the bales of peat moss as they ate their sandwiches. "Having someone not show up on time isn't exactly unusual."

"I know. It's just that this man is so darned cocky about it, as though he owes no explanations to anyone. Why can't he at least call to let us know what's happening?"

"Mrs. Prindle said he did call. He told her they'd try to get there by the end of this week, but that they might not make it until the beginning of next."

"When did she tell you that?"

"Yesterday."

"Why didn't you tell me?"

"I did. I guess you weren't paying attention."

Deeply embarrassed, Letty took a long drink of her soda. Of course Jim had told her that. Craig had even told her that himself the last time she had seen him. What *was* her problem?

She stood, glancing around at the little army of shrubs, each neatly placed in its assigned position. "You're right, Jim. You did tell me, and I'm not paying attention."

He stood beside her. "Why don't you take the afternoon off?" He laughed. "Now there's a turnabout—me giving you some time off. But we have everything under control here, and nothing's about to get done at the Prindles', even if the big equipment is moved in today. Letty, I'm a hard worker, but you make me look as if I'm standing still. Even *you* must have a wear-out point."

"All of a sudden my supply of fathers is multiplying." She grinned and put her hand on his arm. "You know something, Jim, my friend? You're right again. I *am* tired. And you are perfectly capable of finishing up here, so I think I'll take you up on your kind offer of an afternoon off."

She drove straight home, conquering the compulsive urge to swing by the Prindles' to see . . . what, Letty? her nagging mind asked. She had to admit it to herself: She was far more interested in Craig Sullivan's arrival than in a bulldozer and a backhoe and a crane.

All the time she showered and changed into clean jeans and shirt, she fought to still her inner turmoil. Jim's concern had hit home. She was emotionally out of control. The tiger within was awake and trying to gnaw its way out.

She wanted to see Craig. She *shouldn't* want to see him; he was the first man she'd been around in ages who could so quickly and completely unhinge her carefully bolted-into-place temper. It couldn't be healthy to get that mad. So why did she feel more alive than she had in years?

With a sigh, she dropped her work clothes into the hamper. A few less than welcome truths were forcing their way to her consciousness. Temper wasn't the issue. It was just a spillover of all the emotions she had tried so hard for so long to keep securely harnessed.

She dropped onto the edge of the bed, caught in the web of her own thoughts—thoughts that included unwanted memories. For so much of her life she had been not only susceptible but highly receptive to the vitality of the world around her. She'd had no fear of her feelings then. Why would she? Most of her experiences had been joyful, or, at the worst, bearable. Until the first great passion of her life had all but destroyed her.

She jumped up impatiently. She should stop these mental excursions into the past right now, before she opened that memory door wide enough to let some of that awful pain creep through. Shoulds and shouldn'ts—so many of them. She should be satisfied with her life as it was. She had constructed it, step by step, just the way she wanted it. She should be satisfied with her relationship with Duane. She had constructed that, step by step, just the way she wanted it. And the shouldn'ts? Oh boy, she hated to even give them mental space.

This was crazy. If she hung around the house all day, she'd spend the whole time thinking, and that seemed to be lethal. She looked over the note pad by her phone and, without stopping to reconsider, picked it up and dialed one of the numbers written there.

"Hello?"

"Hello, Mrs. Lawrence?"

"Yes."

"This is Letitia Aldridge speaking. I find I have a few free hours this afternoon. Would it be possible for me to take a preliminary look around your place?" Letty, Letty, her mind sentinel scolded, what are you doing?

"Of course! That would be great. My husband happens to be working at home today, and we'll be here until about four. We'd be delighted to show you around."

"Fine. I'll be there within the hour." Letty gathered her pads and clipboard and purse without allowing herself to dwell on who else she hoped would be at the Lawrences' . . . in the vicinity of the dam, perhaps?

She reached the Lawrence home in about thirty-five minutes. It was on a quiet street, with a long, steep driveway that led up to a rambling white colonial with massive plantings that had overgrown their boundaries. Despite all her rubbernecking, Letty could see no sign of a dam or any large construction equipment.

Before ringing the doorbell she took a moment to survey the area. The house stood at the top of a knoll, with a lovely meadow sloping off to one side. The evenness of the terrain and the rich, glossy grass declared that this had once been farmland. By the time she rang the bell her quick mental design board had already sketched four areas of plantings that would benefit from being rearranged and thinned out.

A tall, good-looking woman opened the door. "Hello! You must be Mrs. Aldridge. Come in, I'm Sally Lawrence."

"Nice to meet you." Letty liked her immediately. She had a firm handshake and a no-nonsense manner.

They were joined by Jerry Lawrence, who was also tall and good-looking. She knew after the first few minutes that she'd enjoy working with the Lawrences, and she was forced to send out a silent thank you to Craig for recommending her.

They took her on a tour of the grounds, which were divided by a dirt road that ran all the way to a large barn far to the rear of the house. "The dam is way back in that area," Jerry told her, waving his hand toward the opposite side of the barn.

"Are the men still working there?" She hoped her tone was casual.

"No. They got all the machines loaded onto the carriers and took off just before noon. That was quite an operation. Craig did a beautiful job on the dam. We're very pleased."

Letty should have been pleased, too. Pleased that Sullivan Construction was finally on the way to the Prindles' and that job could get started. It was what she'd been demanding all along. Instead, she was so disappointed to know that Craig had departed that she could actually feel tears welling behind her eyelids. What in the Sam-hill was *wrong* with her? She never cried!

"We bought this place three years ago," Sally was explaining, "and we're restoring it, step by step. As you can see, we'll need your help over a long period of time, but our first concern is getting this herb garden cleaned up."

Letty's mind snapped back to attention. They were standing beside an intricate and extensive herb garden that was snarled and overgrown with weeds. Her heart bumped as she remembered her conversation with Craig about her first garden. He must have known how delighted she'd be to get her hands on this one. "Oh my"—she smiled at them— "this does need help. I'll try to get at it as soon as possible."

Their excitement and pleasure over the fact that she was going to take on the enormous job of getting their grounds in order permeated the rest of the tour, and by the end of it they were on a friendly first-name basis. "And please plan to have lunch with me whenever you can when you're here," Sally enthused. "I'd not only enjoy your company, but I'll pry a few pointers on gardening out of you at the same time."

Letty joined in their laughter, her inner mechanisms almost back to normal. "You've got a deal. Now, where is this famous dam? I'd like to take a look at it while I'm here."

"Sure," Jerry said, looking slightly uneasy. "It's way back in the rear. I could drive you down." He glanced at his wife. "Why don't you get dressed while Letty and I go see the dam. I can throw my clothes on when I come in."

Letty checked her watch. "That's right, you said you had to go out at four. Listen, the most helpful thing for me to do at this point is to wander around on my own and make a few sketches and take some measurements. Then I'll take a walk down to the dam. It can't be hard to find."

"Are you sure? I'd be glad to take you."

"That's absolutely unnecessary. You go on with your plans. I hope you don't mind if I browse around by myself."

"You may roam to your heart's content," Jerry told her. "We'll look forward to working with you."

Letty watched them walk back toward the house hand in hand, and she was just a tiny bit envious of the love they so clearly shared. It revived, for a moment, her vague discontentment.

Letty measured, sketched, and took notes. Despite her resolve not to touch anything, she couldn't resist pulling some of the weeds away from a strangling rosehip bush.

After collecting her data she followed the dirt road to the point where the tractor treads led the way into the woods. The underbrush had been thoroughly flattened on a wide track before her. When she sighted the dam, her first impression was of an enormous quantity of mud, spread out on one side. The dam was rectangular and fairly large. Its small reservoir and stream were also full of water. She wondered how Craig had operated through it. The repair must have been a complete success, because the dam looked solid and neat and permanent.

She made her way through the sweet-smelling brush to the undisturbed side. The surface of the water at that far side was covered by tenacious water lilies that must have hung on through all the disruptions. "You guys are not only invasive," she informed them, "you're practically indestructible."

She sank down on a thick carpet of partridgeberry that grew along the rim of the dam. Letty rarely just rested, but now she did. Both body and mind yearned for quiet, and this was a secluded, inviting haven. She stretched out on her stomach and reached down to dip her hand in the fairly cold water, then plucked one of the fragrant lilies from its pad and raised it to her nose.

"Ah," she murmured to the perfumed flower, "this makes me feel like a wood nymph."

"As I live and breathe, a wood nymph in sneakers."

Startled, she craned her neck to look behind her. Craig stood there, his feet mere inches from hers, his arms crossed, and that teasing smile on his lips. "Craig! What are you doing here?"

"Funny." He lowered himself to sit beside her. "I was about to ask you the same thing."

"Well . . . I had a little time, so I came . . ."

"Never mind. I ran into the Lawrences as they were leaving, and they told me they had just shown you around. Also that you were out here somewhere."

"That explains me. How about you?"

"I wanted to see how it looked after the men took out the machinery."

"You weren't here?"

"No. I was doing some consulting." After a very pregnant pause he asked, "Letty, why did you really come here today?"

She buried her nose in the lily and inhaled deeply, a delaying tactic while she searched for a plausible lie.

"As I said, I had a few hours free, so I decided to use them constructively. By the way, thanks for recommending me to the Lawrences. They're nice people, and I'm going to enjoy restoring the herb garden."

"I thought you might."

She looked over at him, wishing she could do so without experiencing that irritating quickened pulse. He sat there watching her, his legs crossed. He was wearing jeans and a short-sleeve pullover top in a blue that seemed somehow to magnify those eyes. Those eyes that were boring holes into her. Oh, Craig, she wanted to beg, please give me a break—don't look at me.

Enough of this, Letty! her mind chided. She pushed

herself up and started to rise. "Well, it's getting late. I'd better get going."

Craig stood quickly and reached down to give her a hand. Like a fool, she took it. A flash of fire streaked into her arm, skittering through her body. He didn't let go of her hand but simply stood in front of her, very close, his eyes asking questions and his expression displaying the confusion they were obviously both feeling. She pressed her eyelids shut, determined to maintain her equilibrium.

"Letty, Letty." His silky smooth voice caressed her name, sending shivery tingle-fingers over her flesh.

As she lost the war to keep them lowered, slowly, slowly, she raised her eyes to meet his. The impact was physical, jarring her, shaking up all her confusion, churning it into a boiling froth that threatened to whip itself into passion. "Craig...we were going to avoid this..."

"I know. Very wise of us, too. Too bad it isn't going to work."

"But..."

"Why fight it, Letty? You're going to lose."

When he kissed her she could have cried out in relief. Her lips opened under his, parched desert flowers tasting blessed drops of water. She had felt his lips before, but not like this, not with this wondrous feeling of freedom, of time to relish and explore.

The tentative touch lasted mere seconds, then ground into a hungry, demanding grabbing of mouth and mouth. Letty couldn't believe the depth of her wanting. No, not wanting—craving. She craved him, with a need beyond anything she could remember feeling. She opened her mouth, begging him to enter. He did. His tongue was a welcome intruder, boldly crossing the threshold, brazenly asserting its ownership.

She thrust her arms around his neck, hugging his hard shoulders with her hands, pressing against him with an abandon that seemed to belong to someone else.

His arms closed around her, strong, inflexible, unyielding thongs tying her to him. A decision had been made, with no discussion and no opposition. Still bound together, they sank to the thick, cushioning partridgeberry, legs mutually giving way along with resolutions, chemistry reigning supreme.

Letty was exquisitely aware of her flesh. Every tiny cell had leaped to attention; all the bits and particles that made up her body had sprung to life, to deep-breathing, aching, seething life. The cork had popped off the bottle, freeing extravagances of her passionate nature that had been confined for too many years.

There was nothing gentle or timid about this uniting. Letty sank into the welcoming vines with Craig's just-right weight on top of her. She twined her fingers through his silky hair, returning his frenzied kiss with near-violent ardor. His lips felt wonderful on hers; their tongues twisted together in rapacious tasting. She wanted to ingest him, to have him be part of her, and to be part of him.

He raised himself up on his elbows and looked at her. She lay there beneath him, gazing into those morning-glory eyes under their heavy cover of lashes, the handsome, strong face with its straight nose and determined jaw, so close, so deliciously close. His eyes reflected desire, and she decided they must be picking it up from hers.

"Craig," she whispered. "I want you. I want you now."

"Yes," he breathed, his voice rusty and low. His lips met hers again, sweetly testing, nibbling. The tip of his tongue traced their outline, bruising them with softness, quickening her impulses.

He rolled to one side and leaned to kiss each breast through its coating of cloth. Letty moaned. Her nipples seemed to leap forward, straining to pop through the unwanted cover.

With near-wild impatience, Letty helped him unbutton the front of her blouse and undo the wrist buttons, then tug it off, still encased in the cardigan sweater. After that they yanked their own clothes off, never taking their eyes from each other, the intensity of this mutual yearning eliminating all need to tarry with delicacy or trifles. They wanted to be naked—now.

"Oh, Craig, you're so beautiful."

He reached for her. "Isn't that my line?"

"Not anymore." She held him away, wanting to savor each step of this exploration. He *was* beautiful. The lifetime of hard work had honed his muscles, tightened his skin. He was burnished copper already, a skin tone that reflected its kinship with the sun. His broad, well-developed chest was very lightly graced with curly brown hair.

"Letty, every inch of you is perfect. I want them all, all the inches."

His body came to hers with an impact that felt like a clash. Cymbals should sound, she thought. Bells should ring, and drums should roll. She couldn't believe the marvel of his skin against hers, igniting myriad fuses that began to burn toward the final explosion.

The roughened hands with their exquisitely gentle touch began to move over her flesh, feeling, touching, caressing. She ran her hands over him at the same time, her palms tingling with pleasure. He dropped kisses on her shoulder and down her arm, licking the sensitive skin in the crook of her arm. His mouth moved to take her nipple. Letty heaved an audible sigh, cupping the back of his head, encouraging his lips to stay there, to continue doing such devilishly delightful things. He was starting a fire deep within her, a conflagration that threatened to leap out of control.

She ran her fingers over his cheek, touched the eyelids, the fringe of lashes, trying to imprint those visual delights in sensory memory.

He wet her other nipple with his seeking tongue, then pressed it between his lips, the gentle nibbling sending currents of electricity surging through her, shocking to vibrant, vital life her too-long dormant sexuality, until every brain cell in Letty was screaming, "Take me! Take me!"

His lips moved over her stomach and down, just above

the triangle that proved she was a real redhead, then trailed back up to taste the nipples again before rejoining her lips. "Letty..." His tone was a sexy grumble. She raised her head to his, too needful of his mouth on hers to wait the split second for it to arrive.

Oh dear heaven, this was incredible! In every way the reality was better than the fantasy. "Please, please," she murmured deep into his mouth, unable to restrain the plea.

Craig slid fully onto her, entering her swiftly, pushing into her with fierce need. They both gasped, a duet of relief. Letty could feel him there, a hot shaft of delight filling her wild need, feeding her hunger. They pushed together, giving, each to the other in equal share, their passion, untamed and unrestricted.

She could feel the buildup, the internal heaving and rolling, and she wanted it to last forever. But the force took them up, up to the edge, and with a rattling, earth-shaking spasm, over the top. She could feel him come with her to that climax, hear his groan and release with hers. Never, ever, had she experienced anything like it.

They lay entwined, their moisture-slick bodies seemingly glued together. Her legs were wrapped around him; his face was buried in her rumpled hair, his warm gasps of breath brushing her neck. Letty ran her hand over his hair. How lovely. How perfectly lovely to lie here connected to Craig. Craig, her match...oh yes, indeed...and better.

As they lay quietly she realized he must want to hold on to the moment as much as she did. Where had her fear gone? Where had her iron-fisted control gone? Who cared? She didn't miss them at all.

He hoisted himself to his elbows and gazed at her, looking thoroughly content. "I told you so."

"Just couldn't wait, could you?"

"Nope. I like to crow when I'm right."

A smile took possession of her mouth. "It was easy."

"What was?"

"Losing."

"Not painful?"

"Anything but. In fact, if that's what losing feels like, I think I'll take it up as a hobby."

"Good idea. Just smile like that and say 'Yes, dear' whenever we disagree."

"All right."

He laughed, the rumble rippling through her body. "I can just imagine how long that'll last."

She straightened her legs under him, not wanting to disconnect. "Craig..."

"Hmm?"

"That was wonderful."

He had settled back, his head resting beside hers. He raised himself up to look at her again, all hints of joking gone, his expression one of deep sincerity. "Yes. It was better than anything I've ever experienced."

"Really?"

"Really."

"Me, too. So very much better."

"I knew it would be." He eased back down. Neither of them showed any desire to quit their close position. "Kind of scary, isn't it?"

"What do you mean?"

"We've both been circling this like two hawks, afraid we were edging toward something we weren't sure we wanted. Now we're sure we want it, and we, or at least I"—she could feel his silent chuckle—"am certainly in it."

"Are you sorry?"

"No. Are you?"

"No."

"But..." Now he did move, robbing her body of something that had begun to feel like a vital part. "That's no guarantee we never will be."

She studied his face as he sat up. "You sound unsure."

"Letty." He leaned over to kiss her, then reached for his pants. "You and I are both bullheaded people, and we have our lives pretty well structured just the way we want them.

Trying to work this out is going to be some challenge."

She sat up and started to dress, too. "Sometimes I think my father is sending you a script. He called me bullheaded just the other day." She stopped and looked at him. "Are you by any chance a Taurus?"

"I don't know. I've never been very interested in that stuff."

"What's your birthday?"

"May tenth."

"Uh-oh."

"Two bulls?"

"Two bulls."

They were both standing, buckling belts and straightening shirts. As soon as they were clothed, Craig reached over and pulled her into his arms. He just held her, nestled against him, his lips touching her hair for several long minutes while they watched a frog sit on a lily pad, his glassy eyes following a fly that hovered around him. When the silver tongue darted out and the fly became a frog tidbit, they both laughed and started, arm in arm, toward their cars.

"Wasn't it thoughtful of the Lawrences to go away and leave us here alone," Letty commented.

"Mighty nice. They seemed very understanding when I told them we wanted to make love by the dam."

"Craig! You didn't!" She looked at the grin. "Of course you didn't. Although . . . you know something?"

"What?"

"I wouldn't really care."

"I knew it. Under all that veneer of control is a wild, reckless woman." He stopped and turned her to face him. "And I want her."

"Do you?" The two simple words came out in a small, seeking voice. She had been a bit shaken by his assessment of the problems facing them. Her own thoughts voiced by him . . . why did they play back sounding so much more frightening?

"I want you more than I've ever wanted anyone, Letty. There's no question about that. It's just that we're two of a kind, and we could be a pretty combustible mixture."

She flashed him an impish smile. "I'd say there was no question about that."

Craig laughed, taking her hand and continuing their walk. "You're right. No question. Well, now, I'd say the first problem before us is plain."

"It is?" She was sure he was going to mention Duane.

"Yep. Somehow, in our overscheduled lives, we have to find time to spend together, to get to know all about each other."

"Oh dear, you may regret that!"

"No I won't." They had reached the drive where her station wagon and a four-wheel-drive vehicle sat. "Here we are. If I follow you home, can we have dinner together, or are you busy?"

"Oh damn!" She had completely forgotten. "I'm supposed to go to a dinner party with Duane." Chagrined, she stared at Craig. "I'll call and make an excuse."

"No, you'd better go. But Letty . . ."

"Yes?"

"You'll tell him it's off?"

"Yes, I will."

"Call me when you get home."

"It might be late; these people never serve dinner until ten."

"That's okay. If one of the animals answers, be firm. They're very protective of me."

"They'll have to move over. I intend to be invasive."

"I hoped you would be."

She kissed him and got into her car, giving a wave as she pulled out.

She felt the severing all the way to the town border.

Even though it was almost midnight when Letty got home from her date that night, she headed straight for the phone.

She had promised to call. And she needed to call.

There were two rings before Craig's voice, fuzzy with sleep, said, "Hello?"

"Craig? I did wake you up, didn't I. I'm sorry. But I warned you it would be late."

"Who is this?"

"What?" She stopped a hasty identification as soon as she heard the deep chuckle. "That's mean. I thought you'd forgotten me already."

"I'll never forget you."

The words, so softly uttered, with the pure crystal "ting" of sincerity, did more to soothe her fractured nerves than anything else could. "Oh, Craig."

"Did you tell Duane?"

"Yes. I told him I couldn't marry him."

"Was it rough?"

"Yes."

"I'm sorry, honey. I'm sure it hurt both of you."

Honey. He'd called her *honey*. And it wasn't corny or sanguine. It was sweetly refreshing. "Yes, he was very shaken. I didn't tell him about you; that seemed like too much to dump on him at one time."

"What did you tell him?"

"That I cared for him deeply but wasn't in love with him."

"Ouch."

"He knew that, Craig. I've never pretended anything I didn't feel. It's just . . . well, I guess he kept hoping the love would grow."

"I can't blame him for that. I'm hoping for the same thing."

"It's different with you. I'm sure you know that."

"I know."

"Duane said it would be easier for him if we didn't see each other for a while. Luckily, he didn't know how much easier that was for me, too."

"I wish I were there with you, to hold you."

"So do I. I need . . ."

"Go on."

"I feel strange about using the word *need* with you. It's such a demanding word."

"Love is a demanding emotion. It requires a lot of commitment."

Her breath caught in her throat.

"And Letty?"

"What?"

"I think it's right there waiting for us."

"What is?"

"Love."

Her heart rolled over and lay on its back like Pudge did when he was being adorable. She wanted to be adorable for Craig—adorable, adored, adoring. "I do hope so."

"Do you have to work this weekend?"

"I'd planned to."

"Can you unplan it?"

She mentally raced over her schedule. "That's possible. Yes, I could shift things around. What did you have in mind?"

"Could you come to New Hampshire? I'd like to show you my home and introduce you to my animals."

"Not your family? Does that mean your intentions are not honorable?"

"That means that I want you all to myself for now. My family, like the rest of the world, can just wait."

"I could drive up in the morning."

"Good! No, more than that—wonderful." He gave her directions, which she jotted hastily on the phone pad. "The mail box has the number on it."

"Will it be standing?"

"Unless you send some of your young local hoods up here."

"Such harsh language. They think of themselves as pirates of the night."

"I'm sure." The sudden silence hovered. "I hate to say good-bye, because then you'll hang up," he murmured.

"I have to admit that's what I usually do after I say good-bye." She knew what he meant; the thought of cutting the connection made her feel very lonely. "I'll miss you when I do."

"Mmm. Me, too. Letty, I can hardly wait."

"Same here."

They said good night, and she put the receiver in its cradle. It made her feel just the way she had known it would: shut off and isolated and terribly alone.

Letting Duane down had been awful. Letting him down. That seemed such a strange way to put it, yet that's what he had called it. "How can you let me down like this, Letty, when you know how much I need you?"

Did you marry someone, give him your life and your devotion and your body, because he needed you? Did you ask that of someone else when the need was yours? She knew that need was an integral part of love. But at what point did it become a tool of manipulation? And had she once been guilty of trying to use that tool? It was no wonder she had worked so hard to shut off those endless, seemingly unanswerable questions.

She leaned over to pick up Pudge, who had been sitting patiently by the phone table since she'd come in. "Hi, sweet boy. How are you?" She stroked the feather-soft hair. "Do you get lonesome when you're here alone all day?"

Pudge tipped his head up to give her his nose-bump kiss, and she heard the creaky rattle that indicated his purr mechanism was being activated. There had been a time when she would have laughed at the thought that she'd be this devoted to a cat. She had grown up with dogs, one of which had come into her marriage with her. When he had died of old age four years before, she had decided dogs required too much energy for her lifestyle. Actually, she had decided she was better off without a pet.

"You sneaked up on me, didn't you?" She nuzzled the top of his furry head. She had gone to visit a friend, who had shown her a litter of newborn Himalayan kittens. She'd only had to take one look at this one... "Talk about love at first sight! Now that should be a lesson to me. Look how well this worked out." Pudge was such good company. It was sometimes scary to care so much about an animal. Almost as scary as caring too much about a person.

She carried him upstairs and put him on her bed while she got undressed. "Oh, Pudge, I wish I were absolutely sure I did the right thing tonight. It makes me feel so different, so . . . exposed." One nice thing about her conversations with Pudge was that he didn't refute what she said, and he patiently waited through long pauses—like when she disappeared into the bathroom to wash up.

She came back into the room, turned out the light, and crawled into bed, nudging Pudge over to give her more room. She lay there, staring into the darkness, her mind turning and turning. "I said that once, you know, before you knew me. I was beyond hurt; I was demolished. My wonderful, debonair, oh-so-suave husband had been wonderful, debonair, and oh-so-suave with someone else. I stood in our bedroom, in that big, fancy house we lived in, and cried and cried, and I said 'How could you do this to me when I needed you so much?'"

Just remembering that young, vulnerable, aching girl made tears come to her eyes. "And do you know what he said, Pudge? He said he didn't do it *to* me. He did it *for* himself. I hadn't the faintest idea what he meant. But now I think I do. I was asking something of him that he couldn't give. He could never have been faithful to anyone."

She blanched, bombarded by another old enemy . . . humiliation. "And the worst part"—she was whispering now, as though someone might overhear—"is that I always knew what John was like. And I absolutely refused to face it. I lied to myself at least as much as he lied to me. And that's what hurts the most, that I set myself up."

She pulled Pudge up and held him tight. He also didn't seem to mind if she cried into his fur. "You know, I think my daddy was right after all. I've been trying to make myself into something I'm not. I've tried to compensate for having once set myself up by sealing myself off now. Even if this thing with Craig and me doesn't work, things are better this

- 7 -

LETTY WAS WIDE awake by 5:00 A.M. The early-summer sun was still hidden, but its rays were already lightening the sky. She got up and spent far too much time deciding what to wear and what to pack. She felt slightly decadent; she had never gone somewhere to stay with a man who wasn't her husband.

"It's about time," she informed her furry constant companion. "Pretty soon I'll be too old to be wicked." Afraid it was too early to start for Craig's house, she tried to tarry over a cup of coffee. To heck with it, she decided with a grin. She was an early riser, and he might as well learn *all* about her.

Her suitcase was in the car and she was ready to go by seven. She picked up the phone, hesitated, then dialed. Her father was an early riser, too, and he responded to the first ring. "Hello?"

"Hi, Dad." With some reluctance, she explained that she

was going to visit Craig in New Hampshire and asked him to feed Pudge that night and the following morning.

"I must say, Letty, when you kick caution out of the door, you give it a real boot in the fanny. Well, good for you!"

"Dad..."

"Sorry, lost my head. Is there plenty of cat food, or should I pick some up?"

"The cupboard is full of cat food. I've told Pudge that you'll be over to feed him, but he's still sulking."

"I know that cat. He'll talk me into staying there with him or bringing him here."

"Dad, you're worse than I am about that animal."

"You'd better check out Craig's animals while you're there. You may have to keep two houses."

"You're being very premature, Dad. Don't you know you shouldn't count your sons-in-law until they hatch?"

He laughed. "Why, do you think he might 'chicken out'?"

"Ohhhh," Letty groaned. "Good-bye. I left a number by the phone."

"Good. I'll call every fifteen minutes."

"Thanks, Dad."

She hummed a happy tune as she hung up and got her purse and a jacket out of the closet. New Hampshire evenings could turn cold. There was no use trying to say anything but a quick good-bye to Pudge; he was still sulking under the sofa.

The car rolled down the driveway and onto the street. She was on her way! What a strange mixture of anticipation and apprehension she felt. As she drove through the familiar center of town, she fought the temptation to scrunch down in her seat. No one could possibly know that she was off on a rendezvous with a new lover, even if there was anyone around this early on a Saturday.

Letitia Aldridge, her revived little-girl conscience demanded, *what would your mother say?* I don't know, she mentally replied, but my father said to go for it!

It took less than an hour to get to the highway turnoff.

Craig's directions were clear, and she was soon driving through winding countryside that led up gently sloping hills. She almost missed the center of his town, it was so small. But then, so was the center of her town. She parked her car and went into the general store. She didn't really need anything, but she wanted to explore the whole region in which he lived. She wandered around, bought a morning paper, and left.

She walked down the main street, looking into the bakery and the drug store and the post office. By that time she'd run out of buildings to look at. She was procrastinating, and she knew it. With an unsteady stride she returned to her car and started the last leg of the journey.

There were only two more turns to make. She found the sign for Lake Street and made the first of them. What beautiful country! The low mountains were barely more than hills, but they still gave the full effect of hilltops and valleys and sweeping vistas. Lake Street climbed and twisted past several lovely old farmhouses and an unexpected development of nicer than average houses before curving upward through a stand of pine trees.

He eye caught a small wooden sign on the corner of a dirt road. It said simply SULLIVAN with an arrow. She swung the wheel right, and the car climbed up a short, steep rise that leveled off on a ridge. The road followed the ridge for about five hundred feet, then dipped into a slight pocket. The view was marvelous. A cleared meadow sloped off the ridge. It had been mowed just low enough to keep it neat, and there were three enormous ash trees and a spectacular elm in unbelievably good health. At the bottom of the meadow was a lake. "What a location!" Letty breathed.

The road took one more swing to the right, and she saw the house tucked into the hill. It looked comfortable and rustic and permanent. She loved it at first sight.

She stopped her car at the far side of the driveway and got out, glancing at her watch. She hadn't realized how close this was. It was only nine. She hoped Craig didn't sleep late on weekends.

As she approached the house, a lanky brown dog of indeterminate ancestry stood up, stretched, gave three halfhearted barks and sat in front of her, wagging its tail. Letty laughed. "You're some frightening watchdog," she commented, giving the friendly animal a scratch behind the ears.

When she looked up, she saw four eyes surveying her from the roof over the door. The cats were side by side, regarding her with typical feline interest. "Good morning," she said, nodding her head to them.

"I see you've been met by the four-pawed welcoming committee."

Letty whirled around and bumped into Craig, who stood right behind her. "I didn't hear you."

"That's because I snuck up on you. I wanted to grab you before you could get away, and do this." He pulled her into his arms and kissed her, his lips tender and gentle. "Gosh, I'm glad you're here. What kept you?"

"What kept me? I was afraid I was arriving too early." She snuggled into his arms, awed at the magnitude of her . . . what? Relief? Comfort? Happiness at being there.

"You *couldn't* have arrived too early. I've been awake since four o'clock waiting for you." His gaze held hers, sending her numerous messages, all of which she was delighted to receive.

"I thought maybe you slept in on Saturdays."

"I usually do. I sleep until seven or seven-thirty."

Letty chuckled. "One test passed—we're both early risers."

He kissed her again, less gently this time. "I wouldn't care if you slept till noon."

"I wish I could, just once, to see what it's like."

"Where's your suitcase?"

"In the back seat."

He got the overnight bag and led her to the front door. "Oh, by the way," he said, stopping. "You haven't been properly introduced. This is Granny." The brown dog put out a paw.

"How clever! Did you teach her that?" She gave the paw a hearty shake.

"My brother did."

"How come she's named Granny?"

"You can see how old she acts, and she's only four. I figure names should be appropriate." Granny had resettled on the porch in a snooze position. "Take it easy, Granny. Don't exert yourself." Granny gave a wheeze and dropped her head onto her paws.

"And up there"—Craig indicated the two cats still draped over the edge of the roof—"are Careful and Crybaby."

"I won't ask." She said how do you do to the cats, then looked at Craig. "If you ever have children, their names should be fascinating."

His jump-in-and-drown eyes slid sideways to meet hers. "I kind of hope you might have something to say about that."

She could feel the flush skim over her face. Somehow no smart retort came to mind. Craig. His warmth permeated her body, and he wasn't even touching her.

"Come on, let's go in. Have you had breakfast?"

"Just a cup of coffee."

"Good. I got provisions for waffles and bacon and fresh orange juice."

"Oh, does that sound good! What if I'd already eaten?"

"Then you'd have had waffles, bacon, and orange juice for lunch." Laughing together, they went into the house.

They stepped into a rectangular entranceway that was open to the living room. The interior was batten and board paneled with a floor of wide, dark stained wood. The living room was large and obviously furnished more for comfort than show. An enormous rock-face fireplace dominated one wall, and part of the floor was covered by a deep pile wool rug of a pleasing rust color. One whole wall had floor-to-ceiling windows overlooking the lake.

"Craig, it's wonderful."

"Do you really like it?"

"It's perfect. A picture-book retreat." She meant it. As

he showed her through the rest of the house, the impression grew of a man's home—sturdy, comfortable, and warmly receptive.

He left her case in the front hall while he showed her around. "Might as well start in the hub of the house."

They stepped into what had to be the quintessence of the country kitchen—spacious and wood paneled and full of light from the three walls of windows with three lovely views. "Oh, Craig!" Letty exclaimed. "This is beautiful!"

"It was remodeled last year. In fact, *all* of last year."

Letty saw a momentary hardening of his expression. He must have had a battle with the carpenter . . . or the architect? "It took a while, but I finally got it the way I wanted it. I like to cook, so I had this big cooking island put in. It has a regular oven and a microwave and an indoor grill. I got a couple of great big steaks to put on that tonight." He grinned at her, his features relaxing. "And potatoes to bake."

"I'm overwhelmed. You put me to shame; this kitchen is a wonder. I didn't know you liked to cook."

"There's a lot about me you don't know."

"Yes." She couldn't get enough of looking at him. "But I want to know it all."

"Are you sure? You might find some dark corners."

"Well, if I do, maybe I can help air them out."

Craig cupped his hand around the back of her neck, just as he had that first night he kissed her. "That might be very helpful." He stood quietly, his eyes caressing her face. "You have a wonderful face, Letty. So pretty, and so much more. When I first saw you at the Prindles', when you scraped that chair up next to me, all aglow with hurrying and with your beautiful eyes sparkling and alive, I told myself, 'Careful, Craig, she's a Mrs.' I must admit I was glad to find out you were a widow."

She stayed very still, afraid he'd take his hand away from her neck. It sent heated contentment all the way down her back. "Then we were both reacting the same way. You did diabolical things to my sensory receptors."

When his mouth touched hers, she sank into it, realizing

this wasn't just passion. She was falling in love.

Craig went back to get the suitcase, then took her into his bedroom, which she had not yet seen. It was just what she had pictured from the moment she entered the house: big and sprawling and basic. The bed was king-sized—to fit the man, her glowing heart observed.

"This, obviously, is my room. You saw the other two bedrooms and baths. And that, along with an ordinary basement and attic, is it."

"I love it. It's just right."

"Just right for what?"

"For you. It fits you so well. Rugged and masculine and handsome."

He placed her case at the foot of the bed. "And what about you, Letty? Could you and Pudge adjust to this?"

She stared at him, startled by the question. "I don't know. I honestly didn't look at the house that way." An embarrassed smile took hold of her face. "No, that's not so honest. I did look at it that way. I repeat, I love it. It's just right. Are you proposing?"

He laughed, then looked at her, shaking his head. "You're not to be toyed with, are you, Letitia? You're a meat-and-potatoes, put-up-or-shut-up woman. I like that. I like you. And no, I'm not proposing. We have to get acquainted first. I'm a one-step-at-a-time man."

"Well, now that our characters have been defined, how about feeding me? I'm hungry."

"You weren't kidding when you said you liked to eat, were you? I thought maybe bringing you in here would give you other ideas, and you'd throw yourself at me."

"I'll throw myself at you later. First I want to eat and see the grounds."

"Figures. You're only after me because of my acreage. That'll teach me to become involved with a landscape architect."

"Well, your acreage is very appealing."

His eyes were darkening to their smoky hue. "Ease up, lady, or breakfast will be late."

She followed him into the kitchen, grateful that they both seemed to want the same thing: to savor each moment, to take time to cherish every step of the getting-to-know-you process. So much of her life was a rush, she didn't want this to be.

He insisted she play the guest. "This time at least. It may be your last shot at it. Ordinarily it's an 'everyone pitch in and help' operation around here."

She perched on a stool next to the cooking island and observed, fascinated, his expertise in assembling breakfast. He handed her a giant cup of hot, fresh-brewed coffee to sip while she waited. The bacon sizzled on the griddle, and the waffles steamed in the iron. The table by the window was set, and he took two glasses of orange juice out of the refrigerator and carried them over. She enjoyed being pampered; it was a rare occurrence in her life.

"I feel like Queen for a Day."

"Well, don't get too caught up in game shows. You won't get a choice between doors one, two, and three. I'll only offer the one that leads to my room."

"That doesn't distress me one bit."

His eyes met hers. "I'd be disappointed if it did."

They were soon seated at the cheerful, white-linen-covered table, with the delicious aroma of bacon and waffles surrounding them. She didn't say anything until after the first few bites. "This is delicious. I'm impressed. In fact, awed. You're not only a good cook, but white linen and flowers, yet! Go ahead and propose—I'm ready to say yes."

"I want to be sure you're ready to say yes to a lot more than eating."

The waffle almost stuck in her throat. "I thought a few other doubts might have been removed by now."

"Letty . . . careful. You wouldn't want your waffle to get cold."

"Of course not." One thing was certain—nothing else was going to get cold.

He did let her carry the dishes to the sink, where he rinsed them and put them into the dishwasher. "Now we can take a walk and I'll show you my land."

Pride rang in his tone when he said *my land*. He was a New Hampshire man, born and bred, so a deep-felt commitment to his land was natural.

Letty was amazed at how easy being here with him felt. Every minute they had together seemed to magnify his initial attractiveness. This is a fine man, she thought. Ramrod straight and honorable and proud in the New England manner. She hoped . . . no. No projections. As Craig said, one step at a time.

They stepped outside into Letty's favorite kind of day. It looked as if God's angels had been up all night scrubbing his world. She hadn't really noticed how perfect the air and the sky and the visibility were until she walked out at Craig's side. "How much land do you have?"

"Forty-five acres."

"Wow! Does that include that lovely lake down below?"

"It includes about half of it. My oldest brother owns the other half. He lives on the other side."

"I can't see a house."

"No. He built it so we'd both have our privacy. He and Ann have close to seventy acres."

"Is he the brother who works with you?"

"No. That's Jerry. He's married to Elaine, and they have two sons. My across-the-lake neighbor is Glenn. He's a doctor. He and Ann have one daughter. That leaves my younger brother Allan, who's married to a nice girl named Jean. They have a brand-new son."

"Sounds like you never have reason to get lonely."

"I get lonely."

They were walking hand in hand down a path that cut through the woods to the lake. She glanced over at his strong profile, glad to hear one of her own thoughts echoed. "So do I. It doesn't always depend on how many people are around, does it?"

"No, Just who."

For the first time she wondered about that other "who." The woman he had almost married. "Craig . . ."

"Hmm?"

"What was your ex-fiancée like?"

His face tightened again, the way it had earlier that morning. "Evelyn? Slick, elegant, and acquisitive." Somehow Letty got the feeling she would do well to close the subject if she wanted to keep the day bright.

When they reached the lake, they sat on a bench made of a giant log that had been split and sanded and set on two sturdy log ends. "Craig, it's so pretty. You've done a lot of work, haven't you, clearing the woods and cleaning out the brush?"

"Hours and hours. Glenn and I do most of it, along with Ann when she can break free from the house. My other brothers pitch in now and then, but they have places of their own. I've had my men do a few jobs, but I like to see the results of my own labor here."

"I know what you mean. I used to have such a gorgeous garden. It felt good to work on something I wasn't going to walk away from when it was finished."

"Used to? How about now?"

She picked up a twig that had fallen on the bench. "Now I don't seem to have any time to spend on it."

"Sounds as if you work too hard."

Letty burst into laughter. "Heaven help me, my suspicions are true! I accused my father of being in cahoots with you because he's repeating things you've said. Now it's working in reverse."

"I suspect a man could do worse than emulate your father."

"That's a nice thing to say, Craig. I'll pass that on; it'll please Dad."

"He'll think I'm buttering him up."

"That'll please him, too. He likes being buttered up." She stood and gazed out over the sparkling water. "Can we walk around the lake? I see you've made a path."

"Yep. We haven't completed it yet, but it goes to my brother's side. We want to circle the whole lake, but that'll take a while."

"I should think so. What a job." They continued their

stroll. The trees had been cut back from the lake, so the sun bathed them in warm, late-morning rays. Letty pulled off her sweater and tied it around her neck. "I must admit your house surprises me. That and all this beautiful land. I'd assumed all your money and effort had gone into your business. Frankly, I had expected something far less grand."

He fell slightly behind her as the path narrowed. "This *was* far less grand when I bought it twenty years ago."

She turned to stare at him in astonishment. "Twenty years! You must have been awfully young."

"Seventeen. It wasn't exactly a planned purchase. My dad heard about its coming on the market. Glenn had just married, and took a look at it, but it was too run down to interest him. I was with him at the time, and there was something about the place that appealed to me. There were only five acres with it then, and it was dirt cheap. That night at dinner I made the comment that if I had any money I'd buy it."

"Did your folks offer to loan it to you?"

"Nope, better than that. My mother informed me I had more than enough for a down payment. Boy, was I surprised! I'd been working after school and during summer vacations since I was twelve, and I gave most of what I earned to her—I figured I should kick in what I could to help run the house. But she had put it all in a savings account for me. It was amazing how much had accumulated. At that point I didn't argue, since I really wanted the house, so I bought it with a fifteen-year-mortgage that my parents co-signed."

He laughed. "Fifteen years. That sounded like three days past forever at that age, and now I just wonder where the time went. Glenn picked up this property we're now trespassing on, and when the land in between came on the market, we snapped it up."

"Haven't you ever done anything irresponsible?"

"Several things, but I'm not going to tell you about them."

Letty stopped and turned to him. "Dad keeps telling me I haven't spent enough of my life playing, but you make me look like a piker. You've worked hard all your life, haven't you? At least I fooled around a lot in my school years."

Craig chuckled and drew her into his arms. "I guess I never got the hang of goofing off. My two older brothers always had part-time jobs—you know, from paper routes to lawn mowing on up. It seemed natural to me to work. It still does."

"I don't know about this, Craig. The two of us together could be frightening. The work ethic gone berserk."

"I'll tell you what's beginning to sound more frightening."

"What?"

"The two of us apart."

Letty clung more tightly to him, full of wonder at the closeness she felt in so short a time. She raised her lips to his, wanting the closeness extended. His kiss seemed to send hot rays of sun straight through her bloodstream. They seemed so completely in tune, in such total accord. Their brief flashes of competitive confrontation seemed long ago and far away. Surely they would not recur. After all, strong-willed people *should* attract each other.

They walked for a couple of hours. No one was home at his brother's house, but Craig showed her around the house. Glenn's place was larger and fancier than Craig's and had a swimming pool and a tennis court in the back yard. Letty liked the rustic decor of Craig's house better. She could easily have chosen it herself.

He led her through some of the underbrush to show her a spot on the lake where they planned to put a sand beach and another where they had dug an auxiliary hole for a water-lily pond. "We even thought of having a small fishery for breeding trout, but Ann put her foot down. She said that between the two of us, we'd use up every minute we had free from work to work. I think she's right. I have to confess something to you, Letty: It's hard for me to relax."

"Then you're lucky you found me. I'm so low key and laid back I'll be able to teach you the art of relaxation in no time."

"I bet that would get a loud laugh from your father."

"Yes. Of the horse variety."

"At least we'd never be nagging each other about our work habits."

She groaned at his pun but acknowledged the truth of what he'd said. Then, reaching up to touch his lips with her fingers, she said, "You have a wonderful mouth. It always looks ready to laugh."

"Right now it's ready to kiss."

"Now isn't that a coincidence. I happen to have one that's in the same condition."

Craig lowered his lips to hers, pulling her to him, enclosing her in an embrace that was fast becoming an essential haven for Letty. She loved being held by him; it felt secure and safe and homey. Added to the instant sexual excitement his touch elicited, those feelings created a hefty bonding.

The kiss kindled the flame that flickered constantly between them, fanning it to a blazing fire. The wildness of this desire was a new sensation for Letty. She was submerged in it, a more than willing slave to it. She let go of all reserve, responding to her body's urgent demands, responding to her heart's need to be part of this man.

"You know something?"

"What?" Letty turned her head to look at him, lying on his back beside her. They were stretched out on the grass, covered only by a sheet of sunlight.

"If we keep this up, we're bound to land in a patch of poison ivy before we're through."

"Are you intimating that I wouldn't recognize poison ivy?"

"I'm intimating that you didn't take the time to check."

The thought was alarming enough to make her sit up and look around them. "Whew! Safe this time. But in the future, we'd better look before we . . ."

"Before we what?"

She rolled over on top of him and snuggled her face next to his. "You know darn well what."

He put his arms around her, holding her in place. "Aren't

we lucky the summer is just beginning? We can make love in all kinds of places, with just the sky over our heads." He kissed her forehead. "Do you suppose it will work as well for us when we're confined to the indoors?"

"Do you suppose *what* will work as well? Honey, are you trying to tell me something? Do you have a little problem you'd like to discuss?"

"Do I . . . I resent that. What do you mean by *little?*" He gave her bare rear a gentle slap. "And as for any problems . . ."

She kissed his ear and nibbled the lobe. "Excuse me, my error. It's not fair to judge anyone's capacity for endurance before it's put to the test."

"Is that so?" He rolled them over, pinning her beneath him. "Getting pretty sassy, aren't you? In my opinion, what you need is a good—"

"Careful. Don't make threats you can't carry out."

She had gone too far, and that last remark earned her a thorough tickling.

"What are you jumping around for, Letty? Can't you hold still? My, what a madly passionate woman you are—trying to excite me all over again, aren't you?"

"Craig, stop!" She was giggling and writhing too much to effectively fight off the maddening fingers. "I give up!"

"You do, do you?" The tickling stopped, but the writhing went on. She had certainly succeeded in exciting him all over again.

The sun beamed brighter, as though trying to provide more cover for the scandalous scene below.

The rest of Saturday passed in a bright, sun-hazed glow. Letty and Craig talked and talked, about childhoods and relatives, likes and dislikes, learning more and more and liking it.

As they wandered through his somewhat neglected yard, Letty, in spite of her resolution to restrain her instincts for "neatening up," made a number of suggestions for improvement. Craig listened, his polite attentiveness intact, then commented, "Letty, please don't remodel until you move in."

Her mouth flew open for one of her quick comebacks, but a glimmer in his eyes caught her attention. What did she see there? Not anger, or even irritation. But whatever it was made her close her mouth without releasing her retort.

At the end of the day they sat in the cozy living room, cuddled together on the sofa, continuing a pattern that had already formed of staying as close as they could at all times. Letty sipped her scotch and soda and reached for one of the crackers spread with Brie. "I'm almost sorry it's so warm. It must be heaven to have a fire in that fireplace. It looks big enough to heat half of New Hampshire."

She could feel his low chuckle rumble against her back, which rested on his chest. "It sure keeps this room nice and warm. Getting the fire started is the first thing I do when I get home on a winter's night. After working outside all day, it feels good to get thawed out. I've never been much for sitting around and shivering in my own home, so I cut enough wood for the winter and pay the oil bill without complaint."

"Mmm, that's good to know. I'm the hardy type, myself, but Pudge demands a well-heated house. He gets surly when it's cold."

"Speaking of Pudge, you'd better bring him with you the next time you come. He should start getting acquainted with Granny and Careful and Crybaby."

"That should prove interesting. Can you and I stand a weekend of hissing and barking?"

"We can stand anything. Besides, do those gentle creatures appear capable of such carrying on?"

Letty looked at the brown dog stretched out on the carpet, her head resting on one paw, and the two cats curled up beside her. "They're certainly a peaceful sight at the moment, but I've never seen a new animal introduced into a household without a great deal of resistance from all quarters."

"They'll adjust. They'll have to; we won't give them an

option. Besides, Pudge is an indoor cat, and these guys are out most of the time."

"Sounds like a perfect set-up for instant rivalry."

"Nonsense. I'll give them the stock line about love conquering all, and they'll probably throw a welcome party for Pudge."

She laughed. "I can see it now. No, actually I can *hear* it now, full of loud singing, otherwise known as caterwauling."

He kissed her neck. "We'll cross that Rubicon when we reach it. But now . . ." He eased her away from him. "The potatoes must be just about ready. Do you want to toss a salad while I put on the steaks?"

"I'd love to! I was hoping you'd let me cook in your fancy kitchen. If you'd insisted on keeping that to yourself, our whole relationship would have been in jeopardy."

"We can't have that, can we? If you'll feel better, I'll surrender on that one immediately and let you do all the cooking."

"No, that's one contest I don't want to enter. I'm willing to share." They were both unwilling, however, to break their connection, so hand in hand they went to the kitchen.

Preparing dinner was fun. Letty marveled at how an ordinarily mundane job like cooking a meal could turn into a treat. John had never set foot in the kitchen except to get ice for the cocktails.

Everything about being with Craig was fun. It brought to mind a favorite song called "Ain't Love Easy." And it was. It was love, and it was easier than she had ever dreamed love could be. It was more comfortable to be with Craig than with Duane, even though she'd known Duane for so many years and Craig for so few weeks.

They ate dinner by candlelight in the charming, wood-paneled dining room that opened off both the kitchen and the living room. Steak and potatoes, always Letty's favorites, had never tasted so good to her before. Each succulent bite seemed enriched by the pungent seasoning of love-herbs. Their eyes clung across the flickering light, their knives cutting the meat, their forks finding their mouths in the miraculous Braille of lovers.

Much, much later, in the middle of the night, Letty awoke suddenly, frightened by an unfamiliar sound. For a moment she couldn't remember where she was, until the sweet-hot feel of her skin against Craig's pushed recognition through the fog of sleep.

How exquisite, she thought, lying tucked against his body. How had she made it into her mid-thirties without discovering the depth of her passion? She breathed deeply, inhaling Craig's pleasing scent.

He slept soundly and silently on his back with his head inclined toward her. She looked at her hand, lying on his chest, the fingers curved as though, even in sleep, they had been determined to hold on to him.

Craig, Craig, her mind whispered, how empty my life was before you came into it. How could I have been so oblivious to the void? I love you. I love you wildly and sweetly and with a need I never knew I had.

She tried to remember how it felt to be Letty Aldridge, engaged to marry Duane Winter. The memory fuzzed and wavered, receding from recollection. That woman was someone else, surely. Someone whose blood ran smooth and chill, instead of racing in white-hot streams. As she bid the swiftly departing ghost good-bye, she experienced a strange twinge of fear. The alarmingly alive Letty Aldridge who was lying next to Craig Sullivan was, without question, far more vulnerable than the one disappearing from mental sight.

She didn't want to fall back to sleep right away. She wanted to examine more minutely this encompassing sense of emotional rebirth, but all too soon the drowsiness of impending slumber overtook her, and she slipped off into a dream.

- 8 -

THE PHONE INTERRUPTED their late Sunday brunch. It was Craig's brother, who was in Vermont setting up for a site-development job.

"I have to go, honey," Craig told her when he put down the phone. "Jerry thought he had a firm contract on this, but they're giving him some trouble. I'll have to take another look at what we'll run into when we excavate for the lake."

"A whole lake?"

"Yep. It's a big job, and it could be a big mess. We need either a set contract price that allows for the possible problems, or a cost-plus contract. We'll give them either one, but not what they want, which is a set price that *doesn't* allow for any problems."

"Can't blame them for trying."

"I can when it takes me away from you."

"You can't go in the morning?"

His eyebrows went up. "Too risky. There's a redheaded landscape architect who might get downright mean if I don't

128

show up at the Bartholemew Prindle house in the next few days."

"What if she gave you a slight extension?"

He laughed and pulled her toward him. "Wouldn't help in this case. I can't afford to have my men in Vermont just hanging around for a whole day. Jerry says we can see these guys tonight, and either we'll strike a bargain or we'll pull our equipment out and send it to the next job."

"Just like that?"

"Just like that. One thing I don't like is having someone welch on a deal."

"That's two things. You also don't like to be ordered around."

"You're right, that's two."

She put her arms around his neck. "All right, you wonderful, sexy hunk, I can take a hint. I'm getting booted out already. You've tired of me in less than two days..." His lips put a stop to her silliness. As the kiss ended she sighed in contentment and said, "You know, honey, if you run into a short delay, don't worry about it. I can tell your men where to start digging."

"My men know what they're doing. If I can't get there, I'll make sure they're kept informed."

She pushed her chair back. "Have you pointed out the importance of skirting the garden areas?"

"I have pointed out where the garden areas are supposed to go and asked them to stick as close as possible to the plan. If a minor problem arises, they use their best judgment. If a major problem arises, they ask me."

"I'd rather they checked with me if you're not there, Craig. After all, I *am* the one who has the responsibility to coordinate everything."

"Letty, my part of that job is under my supervision. Period."

She tried to keep her tone light. "I thought we'd agreed that I was to oversee the project."

"Any such agreement was made by you, with yourself."

"Craig! Dammit! The landscape architect is *supposed* to

have overall control. You simply cannot ride roughshod over my plans!"

"Control. That word seems to pop up a lot." That "back off" look was showing up in his eyes, but she ignored it. "Letty, I'm not riding roughshod over anything. You're the one who keeps inventing one problem after another before they have time to happen. All I want to do is what I contracted to do. Dig the pond and dig the swale the way they should be dug, under *my* supervision, at which point my machinery will leave the area and you can plant an English garden, a Japanese garden, and a Malaysian jungle, for all I care!"

"And just how are you going to supervise what your men are doing in Sherborn, Massachusetts, if you're way the hell up in Vermont?"

"Who said I would be? I just told you I was going to Vermont now so I could get to the Prindles' on time. Letty, why are you creating problems?"

"Me? All I said was that I wanted to keep an eye on what's done on my job, that's all."

"Then do so. Just remember what's yours is yours and what's mine is mine."

"Nice. Is that how you'd feel about marriage, too?"

"How in the devil did marriage get into this?"

"I don't know, it just cropped up." She jumped up from the table and started to transport the dishes to the sink. "You're so tight-fisted with your supervisory rights I was afraid it might be a trait that cut straight through your character."

Craig stood and brought the cups over, banging them down on the counter. "And how about you, Letty? Is your compulsive need for control likely to extend to me? Because I'll tell you here and now, I will not allow you to run my life or my business."

"I'd better go pack."

"Might be a good idea."

She stomped into the bedroom, fuming with righteous indignation. After all, what had she said? Simply that she wanted to help him out by keeping an eye on his men in case he was detained in Vermont. He should be grateful instead of so blasted pigheaded! She grabbed her suitcase out of the corner, whacked it down on the bed, and proceeded to stuff her few pieces of clothing in. "Ungrateful lout," she mumbled, throwing yesterday's jeans into the case.

Craig strode into the room, came straight to her, and grabbed her by both shoulders. "Why do you do that?"

"Do what?"

"Keep trying to turn what should be a fairly simple job into some kind of power struggle. You know damn well I never agreed to let you tell me or my men how to do our work."

"That is *not* what I am doing! I don't understand how you can take the position that what you're doing has nothing to do with what I'll be doing. It all ties in together!"

"Have I told you what to plant?"

"No."

"I rest my case." He dropped his hands and crossed to the closet to pull out a duffle bag.

"It's not the same thing, Craig. Even you should be able to recognize that! I have to plant around what you dig. You don't have to dig around what I plant."

"Oh? I thought that's what you were trying to make me do."

"I was asking for some slight degree of consideration for the problems I'll run into if the creek and the pond aren't done right."

"Aha! So there it is! If Letitia Aldridge, the genius of landscape architecture, doesn't tell me exactly how the job should be done, I'm bound to screw it up. At least we're getting right down to basics." He slammed some work boots and a heavy sweater into the duffle.

"You're the one who's blowing this all out of proportion. You haven't compromised on one single thing yet! The pond is being dug when *you* want to do it, in the shape *you* want to make it. There will be no incline behind the pond because

you don't want to do it. The message so far is loud and clear. You think everything you're doing is far more important than what I have to do!"

"There's a reason for that."

"Oh? Then perhaps you'd be kind enough to tell me what it is."

"Because it's true. My part of the job *is* more important."

Letty almost slammed her finger in her suitcase. Her breath was coming in short gasps, and she could feel the blood rushing to her face. "Of all the conceited . . ." She faced him squarely, her hands on her hips. "I bet this would all have been different if I were a man!"

His eyebrows shot up. "Some things would sure as hell have been different."

"Oh!" Her foot stamped, all by its stupid self. "If that isn't just like the typical macho man—when in doubt, bring sex into it."

"I didn't exactly bring sex into it all by myself." Craig went into the adjoining bathroom and returned, stuffing a few toilet articles into a small bag. "And quit trying to turn this into some feminist-versus-male-chauvinist diatribe. That has nothing to do with it, and you know it."

"Is that so? Then just what *was* the reason for your cute little remark about your work being more important than mine?"

"Plain fact, that's the reason. I move terrain around. If it isn't done right, the result can be flooding or filling in or stagnation, any of which can be destructive to the surrounding area. If *you* make a mistake, it just won't look as pretty."

"Why you pompous ass! Of all the condescending attitudes! *Pretty!* What a demeaning word! Why, when I'm through, that property will be stunning! It will be spectacular! It will be—"

"Monumental?"

"Oh!" Letty jerked her suitcase off the bed, forgetting that she hadn't secured the fasteners. The lid few open, spilling everything onto the floor. "Dammit!" she shrieked, dropping to her knees to push her scattered belongings back into place. As she picked up her second slipper she heard an unbelievable sound. Laughter. That insufferable man was laughing at her! She looked down at the slipper in her hand and, without further thought, threw it at Craig.

He ducked and laughed louder. She threw the other slipper, then rummaged angrily through the case looking for something else to throw. Her hand closed around one of her gum shoes. She pulled it out and heaved it.

"Ouch! Dammit, Letty, that hurt!"

"Good! You deserved it!" She realized, too late, that the second gum shoe was in her hand in hurtle position. Before she could rethink the move, Craig was on her, his hand closing around her wrist.

"Knock it off, you crazy wildcat! What you need is a good spanking."

"Don't you dare! You said you never hit a lady!"

"What does that have to do with hitting you?"

"Craig! Let go of me!" She fought, to no avail, to free her hands.

"Why, so you can bash me? How come it's okay for you to hit me and not okay for me to hit you?"

"I'm a woman!" She could almost hear the trap spring shut behind her as the words left her mouth.

"Aha! So now you're hiding behind your gender. What happened to equality?"

"Craig, you let me go. Your brute force is not appreciated!"

"No? What *do* you want, another spineless wonder like Duane?" He let go of her wrists, and she sat back on her heels, glaring at him in outrage.

"Is that your interpretation of a gentleman?"

"No. Of a puppy dog masquerading as a man." He was squatting on the floor in front of her, almost nose to nose.

"I gave up Duane for you. I'm beginning to think that was a mistake!"

Craig's face had an ominous reddish glaze. "That's very interesting. I thought you gave him up for yourself, as well. Don't do anything just for me, Letty. That *would* be a mistake. As a matter of fact, maybe Duane is just right for you after all, if you want someone who'll wag his tail and lick your hand when you speak."

"Why you . . ." She watched, horrified, as her own balled-up fist shot through the air into Craig's chest. Before she could tell him she didn't mean it, she was flat on her back, pinioned to the floor. "Craig, I . . ."

His face glowered above her, the dark lashes lowered, the strong jaw set. She felt a moment's apprehension, followed by a wave of momentous desire. "Craig, I . . ." Her voice had fallen to a whisper.

His lips crushed down on hers, bruising in their demand. The weight of his body pushed her back to the hard wood floor. The minute he let go of her hands her arms flew around his neck in instant surrender to her rampaging wants. And oh, did she want. Savagely, wantonly, rashly. The anger that was rushing through her bloodstream had turned to lust, inflaming her veins, carrying the craving in mad-dash haste to every segment of her being.

Their lips ground together, punishing with sweet violence, chastising with exquisite ferocity. She felt the imprint of the neck-to-ankle zipper on her dressing gown stenciled into the flesh between her breasts. Craig raised himself on one arm and pulled the tab, opening the way to her bare breasts. He slid down to take one of the nipples in his mouth, sucking it in to meet his tongue.

"Ohh . . ." It was half gasp, half groan, and it had come from her. She arched her neck and stretched her toes, creating greater distances for her ecstasy to travel. Her fingers twisted in his hair, pillaging the softness of the strands, reveling in the delight of their feathery caresses.

Craig had slid down even further and was creating havoc with her careening senses. His mouth and tongue, the most invincible of invaders, conquered, inch by inch, her eagerly surrendering flesh.

There was nothing else, no past, no future, nothing but this consuming moment, commanded by her rapacious longing for more touching, more kissing, more feeling. He was above her again, his hungry mouth on hers. She reached for the buttons on his shirt, desperate to bare his skin. Her fingers fumbled and failed. With impatience born of her need, she tore at the garment, pushing it from his shoulders, running her hands greedily over his taut skin.

He loosed one hand to unfasten his shorts and force them down his legs. Then he was in her, his pressing ardor grinding her buttocks into the unyielding pine boards. "Oh, Craig!" she gasped. "Yes, yes, yes . . ."

There was no vestige of control left to her. She was caught up in the whirling frenzy of his lovemaking, imprisoned by her unquenchable appetite for him. She shoved her body against him, hearing the low growl of his pleasure.

Her fingers curved into his hard buttocks, compelling him closer, closer, closer than was possible. She felt all the tides of every ocean rising in her, curling in extravagant waves, whipping her around and around until, with a last mighty heave, she was tossed skyward, her body arching in the hot sun. The voice of her lover followed her, crying, "Letty, Letty!"

They lay entwined, breathing in unison. Even the slick film of sweat that melded their bodies together was a sensual treat. She realized that the fingers of one hand were tangled so tightly in his hair that it must be painful. She loosened her hold. "I'm sorry," she whispered. "Did I hurt you?"

"Yes," he rumbled in her ear. "Please be more gentle next time."

"Oh you . . ." She heaved her hips.

"Mmm. Do that again—it feels great."

"Craig," she murmured.

"What?"

"Nothing. I just wanted to say your name."

He propped himself on one elbow, his chin on his palm, and looked at her. "Not mad anymore?"

"Uh-uh. I think I used up all my vital juices on other emotions."

"That's good. Now I know why there's so much hoopla about fighting and making up. When we start living together I estimate our remaining life-span at about three and a half years. But we'll go out smiling." With that he pushed himself up to a standing position and offered her a hand. She hated to move, but she did.

"I suppose you have to get started for Vermont." She sorted out some underwear, a clean pair of jeans, and a top from the heap on the floor.

"Unfortunately, yes. I've got to get to that meeting. Why don't you use this bathroom; I'll go to the other one."

She watched him turn to leave the room. "Hey, just a minute." She walked to him and, standing on tiptoe, slid the tip of her tongue into the cleft of his chin. "I was right, it just fits."

His eyes, dark blue with happiness, held hers. "And what was that all about?"

"Just answering a question I asked myself the first night we went out to dinner."

"I see. I've answered most of my questions, too. We'll have a mutual one to consider before long." She wanted him to put it into words, but he just winked and said, "When we get to know each other, of course."

All too soon she was getting into her car to go in one direction, and he was getting into his to go another. She felt strangely frightened by the impending separation. The fear felt old, as though it belonged to another time.

As she headed home, she hugged tight all the memories of the short weekend, going over and over each one as she drove. She did feel like a sixteen-year-old, light-headed with her first crush, unhampered by adult responsibilities. She was wildly in love with a man she hadn't even known until a couple of months ago. On an impulse she leaned her head toward the open window and shouted, "I'm in love!"

No one could hear her on the busy highway, but she didn't care. She just felt like announcing it. "I'm happy!" she yelled to the nonexistent highway audience. She felt blatantly, deliciously decadent. "Up with wickedness, down with decorum!" It was fun to shout at the top of her lungs, and she knew she'd better get it out of her system before she reached her own town, where it would certainly *not* go unnoticed.

"Craig." That came out as a whisper. A happy, lovesick, spoony-moony whisper. She had fallen in love with the blue-eyed pond-digger. Her earth had moved.

When she reached home, reality hit her with a resounding slap. The phone was ringing as she entered the house, and she managed to get to it before it stopped. "Hello?"

"Sounds like I caught you running in the door."

"You did. Hi, Jim." It was her assistant.

"Letty, we have a problem. Len pulled a back muscle water-skiing at the Cape yesterday. It appears he'll be laid up for a while."

"Oh no! Will he be all right?"

"He'll be fine," Jim assured her. "He just needs lots of bed rest."

"Hmm. Do we know how long he'll be laid up?"

"Yeah. Two or three weeks."

"Good gravy! What're we going to do? Don't answer that; we both know already. Have you called any of the other men?"

"I called all the guys who've worked with us on and off and any others I knew about. Naturally, they're all busy."

"Naturally. There's never a spare hand anywhere at this time of year. Well, that's that. We'll do the best we can. I'll get in touch with the Bakers to let them know we probably won't get to them until next week."

"At the earliest."

"At least all those trees are out, and the roof will have a chance to dry."

"It'll probably go into shock from its first exposure to the sun. What do we have left at the Fraziers'?"

"The pool area is done, and the screening plants are all set, so that leaves the rest of the front, the path, and the back of the house."

"The soil is pretty well prepared, but that's still a lot of work."

"Amen. Jim, any chance you could work next Sunday as well as Saturday?"

"I've already planned on it. So has Sam."

"I love you both."

"You should be more discriminating, Letty. We're both bums, you know."

"I know, but what can I do?"

They laughed together and hung up. The banter went on all the time with the guys she worked with. They were good friends. She reached for the phone to call Len to check on how he was doing. His line was busy; she'd have to call later.

She stared at the phone, struck by a new realization. She had to work next weekend, so she wouldn't be able to spend it with Craig. The thought was devastating. "You *always* work on weekends," she reminded herself. So many things to take a fresh look at, to rearrange.

She picked up her suitcase and started upstairs. Where was Pudge? If he wasn't right there to greet her, it meant that her father must have taken him to his house. As she climbed the stairs she found herself noticing other things: the comforting way it felt to be heading to her own room, the familiar pictures on the wall. Her fortress, so carefully built against . . . what? Someone like Craig Sullivan? Her bastion had been stormed, and the invasion was successful.

A strange, chilling wave of fear swept through her. She stopped dead, shaken. How silly. Hunching her shoulders to release the sudden grip of tension, she proceeded upstairs.

The feeling persisted as she unpacked her suitcase. Something had flown loose inside, some long-caged emotions had broken free and were flying high. She hadn't had that sensation since . . . since she was twenty years old and John Aldridge had finally asked her for a date. That time the drop to reality had been precipitous, the crash almost fatal.

She moved hastily to the upstairs phone to call her father. After four rings, she was beginning to wonder if he was home. Then he answered.

"Hi, Dad. I'm home."

"Letty! I'm glad I came in when I did. I just walked in. I've been out fertilizing the fruit trees."

"Atta boy, Dad. Keep them healthy. How's my cat?"

"Spoiled, demanding, lazy. The same as ever."

"Good. Is this a good time for me to come get him?"

"Yes. Perfect. Have you eaten supper? I have two immense lobsters. Want to share the bounty?"

"Have you ever known me to refuse lobster?"

"Never."

"I'm not about to change my habits now."

"Are you sure?"

The unexpected question stopped her. "Tell you what. I'll address that one when I get there."

"Fine. I'll put the water on to heat. See you soon."

Letty arrived at her father's house about thirty minutes later. She slowed the car to a crawl as she drove into the curving driveway. For the first time in years she really looked at her surroundings, the beautifully lush green lawn that swept up to the gracious white colonial with the black shutters. It was so familiar. It made her feel, just as it had when she was a child, safe.

A disturbing jolt of her earlier wave of fear shook her. She liked to feel safe. Safe and secure and under control. The exultation that had accompanied her on the drive home from New Hampshire had vanished. But why? She shrugged off the troubling question as she opened the back door and hollered "I'm here!"

Pudge ambled out of the kitchen and rubbed against her ankles, purring loudly. "Hi, handsome!" Letty bent to pick him up. "Have you been a thoughtful guest?"

"Hi, Letty," her father called. "Come on in."

She entered, gave her father a kiss, and pulled a chair away from the table. "I'll sit for a minute so I can pet you-know-who, then I'll help you cook."

You-know-who gazed up at her with his wide knowing eyes and meowed. It felt good to be here with her dad in the kitchen she'd known since her childhood, with Pudge's familiar weight on her lap.

"You don't need to help. The water's boiling, so I'll just throw in the lobsters, and everything else is ready." He brushed his hands together and smiled. "How about some white wine?"

"Sounds good." She watched him perform his ritual of taking the wine out of the refrigerator, studying the label as though he'd never seen it before, uncorking the bottle, sniffing the cork, then pouring a taste into a glass to sample.

"Ah, that's fine." The pronouncement came as though

he was surprised the wine was acceptable. He poured some into two wineglasses and handed her one.

She grinned at him. "Tell me, Dad, have you ever opened a bottle of wine that wasn't fine?"

"No, but I keep hoping. I did get to send one back at a restaurant once." He dropped the lobsters into the water, set the timer, then pulled a chair up next to hers. "Now, how did the visit to New Hampshire go?"

"Such restraint. I expected to be pummeled with questions the minute I walked in."

"I'm practicing verbal temperance. Now, now, don't keep me waiting. How did it go?"

"You're worse than a nosy girlfriend!" She grinned at him, then looked down at her hand that was stroking Pudge's fur. She had a sudden, vivid recollection of how that hand had looked lying on Craig's bare chest—and how it had looked balled into an angry fist.

"You're looking pensive. Is anything wrong?"

Her eyes swung to his. "Oh no. My mind was wandering, I'm afraid. I guess the best way to tell you what happened is to let you know that you were right all along. Craig is not only *a* match for me, I'm quite sure he's *the* match for me."

Caleb nodded his head, more sober than she'd have expected. "I rather thought so. Just something about him . . . probably his eyes. They're just like Pudge's, and I know how hung up you are on that cat."

She glanced down at her furry friend. "Now that you mention it, you're right. I wonder if that does have something to do with the attraction." She looked up into Caleb's twinkling eyes, and they both laughed.

"Well, I'm delighted. I can't tell you how glad I am to see you getting interested in someone with a real backbone. Speaking of the opposite breed, have you alerted Duane to this turn of events?"

"Yes. I wouldn't go this far without telling him. That would hardly be fair."

"True. Although"—he got up to check the lobster and put the salad on the table—"if you caught Duane in the middle of a golf tournament, he probably wouldn't notice anything was amiss in any case."

"Dad . . ."

"All right, sorry. I *am* far too critical of Duane. With an ordinary, run-of-the-mill woman, he'll be fine. But with you . . . well, I hate to see a grown man led around by the nose."

"How do you know I can't do that with Craig?"

Caleb had lifted the lid of the kettle, and he looked at her through the rising steam. "You know something, Letty? I'd give a lot to be there the first time you tried it."

"You already missed it."

Her father plucked the lobsters out of the boiling water with the tongs. "Darn. How did that go?"

"Don't ask."

During dinner, amid the cracking of claws and dipping of succulent lobster morsels into melted butter, Letty told him about Craig's house, and what she had learned about his family. Everything she told him increased the expression of satisfaction on his face. But when she mentioned that Len had been injured and she had to work both days of the upcoming weekend, the lines in his forehead deepened. "You work too hard." Letty chimed in for the last of the statement. They looked at each other and laughed again.

"Would you believe Craig told me the same thing? I accused him of being in cahoots with you."

"Oh? And what did he say to that?"

"That a man could do worse than to emulate my father."

Father and daughter looked at each other fondly, the love between them a warm and vital presence. "That's a very nice compliment. But then, if a man has the good sense to fall in love with my daughter, I suppose it shouldn't surprise me that he'd have the good sense to appreciate a sterling-grade potential father-in-law."

"Duane fell in love with your daughter."

"Strike the above."

Caleb quietly studied her face for a moment, then asked, "Letty, are you sure there's nothing bothering you?"

She stared at him, startled by the question. Then she

lowered her eyes. "No, I'm not sure. Something *is* troubling me, and I can't put my finger on it."

"Do you suppose you might be a little afraid of falling in love?"

She gave him a weak smile. "That's silly. Everyone wants to fall in love."

"Well, that's the party line, at least."

"Dad, what are you trying to say?"

"Letty, I've watched you, little by little, over the course of at least the past eight years, lock away some seventy-five percent of your emotional fire."

"I should think you'd welcome that. You're always after me about my temper."

"Unfortunately, *that* you didn't lock away. Besides, don't confuse a volatile temper with what I'm talking about."

"Then what?"

"Your defiant spirit. The way you challenged fate, the way you demanded fairness from life."

"That was pretty silly, wasn't it? Most of the time life *isn't* fair."

"True. But you never accepted it quietly. Not until that—" He stopped, dropping his head for a moment, obviously composing himself. "Not until John knocked the stuffing out of you."

She watched him, really aware for the first time how much he must have suffered through all the awfulness that had engulfed her. How blind children could be to the pain of their parents, she thought. "Dad, why are you telling me this now? I thought you were pleased by my attraction to Craig."

"Letty, my dear, I am more than pleased. I'm excited. You've cracked open the box that has imprisoned all those exuberant emotions, and I'm hoping—no, more than that, I'm praying—that you throw the lid away and let the real Letitia stand up."

"You saw it, didn't you? You recognized what it was before I did."

"What's that, honey?"

"How scary it is for me to open that box."

"Why wouldn't it be? You gave your heart away before it even had time to grow to full size. How were you to know that John wasn't really a man, just an oversized boy?"

Letty turned her wineglass, fighting down the rise of tears. "It's so frightening, Dad. It's as if something wild had been turned loose in me. And I was thinking, when I came in, how safe and familiar and comfortable this house felt, and how appealing that is."

"Hmm. But for me, this house, as well as everything else in my life, lost much of its safety and familiarity and comfort when your mother died. There's no substitute for love, Letty. Real man—woman love, full of fire and ice and fighting and making up and ups and downs and, most of all, sharing. You haven't had that yet. I was afraid you never would. If there's a chance of it with Craig, grab it and don't let go!" He stood and came to her side, putting his arm around her shoulder. "You look tired, honey. Go on home and rest. I'll do the dishes."

"Okay, I'll take you up on that. I've got an unbelievable week ahead." She stood and put her hand on his arm. "Dad, thanks."

"Your happiness is all that matters to me."

"I know. That means a lot. It always has."

She put Pudge in his cat box and carried him out to the car. For just a moment she gazed pensively at the front of the house she had grown up in. She had the weirdest sensation of tearing herself away from a known haven, very similar to what she'd felt when she first went away to school.

She got into the car and started it, then headed for her own home. Her own home. What would that be a year from now?

- 9 -

THE TELEPHONE RANG SHRILLY. Letty groped for the offending instrument, trying to lift her eyelids and struggle out of the dream in which she had been so involved. "Hullo?" she croaked.

"Hello." The voice on the phone was wide awake, chipper, and female. "Is this Letitia Aldridge?"

"Uh-huh."

"This is Caroline. I'm the secretary for the Sullivan Construction Company. Craig asked me to call and let you know that the G 1000 Grade-all is at the Bartholemew Prindle property and that one of the men will be digging there by six-thirty this morning." There was a pause, during which Letty tried to imagine what a Grade-all 1000 might be and why a secretary would be calling in the middle of the night. "I was looking at the note, but it doesn't say what will be dug, so I guess you know." The woman gave a cheerful chuckle.

Letty struggled harder to surface. "What time is it?"

"It's five twenty-five. I hope I didn't wake you up. Craig said you were an early riser."

"Yes, right." She tried to sound like an early riser. Just then her alarm went off. She fumbled with the small clock, finally locating the "off" button. "Are you in the office at this hour?"

"No, I don't get to the office until eight, but Craig phoned last night and asked me to be sure to call you first thing. He said you liked to be kept informed."

Letty swallowed the retort that rushed to mind. He probably thought this was funny. "Yes, right," she repeated. Suddenly the message registered. "This morning? They're starting this morning? Are you sure?"

"That's what the note says. Also . . ."

"Also?" She had a foreboding of impending doom.

"Craig will be moving the crane into place later today and will dig the pond tomorrow."

"What?" Her squealing voice cracked in mid-syllable.

"That's right. Let's see if there's anything else. No, that's the whole thing."

That was quite sufficient. "I thought Craig was in Vermont."

"He was, but he planned to leave first thing this morning to drive to your area. He says he has to get the equipment to Vermont by the end of the week."

Dear heaven, how could she shove one more thing into her day? "All right, thanks for calling."

"You're welcome. Have a nice day!" Caroline of the up-and-at-'em sunshine voice hung up.

Letty pushed her body out of bed. What day was it, anyway? She'd been so completely lost in dreams she was having problems with orientation. Monday. It was only Monday. Craig had told her that, at best, the creek digging wouldn't start until Tuesday, and he couldn't get to the pond before Wednesday or Thursday. Today was impossible; it was more than full, it was jam-packed. What the devil was she supposed to do? Drop all her other commitments to conform to what was convenient for the Sullivan Construction Company? Still grumbling, she headed for the shower.

"He can't kid me," she snarled at Pudge twenty minutes later as she put his breakfast food on a plate. "He didn't want me hanging around while the digging was done in the first place. He probably knew darn good and well that they'd be in there by today!"

"Meow?"

"What?" She looked down at the dish, still in her hand. "Oh, sorry." She set the plate on the floor and poured herself a glass of orange juice. She'd better not even take time to make coffee. She was due to meet Jim and Sam at the Fraziers' at six-thirty. There was no way she could stop at the Prindles'. Maybe she could zip over at noon. What a pain.

"Dammit!" she yelled, stamping her foot.

"Rreowww!"

"Oh! Oh, Pudge, I'm sorry. I didn't mean to step on your tail."

Pudge glared at her from his retreat under the table, his ears plastered back, his eyes wide and fierce.

"Oh..." Laden with guilt and still simmering with frustration, Letty grabbed her supplies and headed out the door.

The morning was one long, continuous disaster. The metal strippings she had ordered for the edge of the Fraziers' walk weren't done, so she and the two men had to change their plans to finish the path and tackle the landscaping of the front of the house instead. They ran into a huge boulder right where the crab apple tree was to go, which meant getting in touch with Roger Jenkins and talking him into bringing his backhoe over to dig it out. Then the other work was hampered by the fact that nothing could be planted where the machine had to come in.

Just before noon Letty decided to take a run over to the Prindles' to see how things were going, but a truck arrived to deliver the metal strips, followed closely by two truckloads of pea-stone gravel for the walk. She worked for half an hour with Jim and Sam to curve the metal strips to the right contour, with no success. Finally she said, "Jim, you and Sam take them up and curl them around the water tank by the pool. That should give us just the right bend."

The gambit worked, and by four-thirty that afternoon the metal strips were in place, the gravel distributed, the boulder removed, and the crab apple tree planted. Letty was wiped out. With a weary wave she got into her car, her spirits almost as heavy as her gait.

She headed toward the Prindles'. Her heart leaped at the prospect of seeing Craig at the same time her mind churned over her frustration at the arbitrary way he had shifted schedules around. She liked order and precision in her life. She liked things under control.

Her brain snapped to attention at that thought. Then why was she getting further and further entangled with a man who sent her control mechanisms into total, chaotic malfunction? She was too tired, just too tired to grapple with that one.

The moment she stepped out of her car in front of the Prindle house, her ears were assailed by an unbelievable racket: the grinding and clanking and banging of metal, underscored by a grating squeal. As soon as she got to the side of the house she could see the crane inching its way across sections of planking, or what Craig had referred to as pontoons or mats, that were laid out in front of it.

Letty stopped to study it. The machine resembled a gigantic metal praying mantis. The sixty-foot boom stretched its rigid neck to the sky, dangling a long cable that held a huge bucket at the bottom. The green housing squatted on a wide base with enormous treads.

She watched in fascination as the huge machine reached the end of its improvised platform and stopped. The cabin swung full circle, and the hook on the bottom of the bucket latched onto the cables that held the three sections of heavy planking that formed the pontoon, swung it off the ground with a clank, rattle, and crunch, swung around again, and repositioned the pontoon in front of the machine. When all the mats were moved, the crane slowly chugged forward once again, stopped, and repeated the operation. The procedure had to be followed all the way across the wide lawn to preserve the grass. No wonder it took a full afternoon to move the crane into position!

As the housing swung around again, Letty waved, and the motor slowed to idle. Craig eased himself out of the cab, jumped down to the ground, and headed toward her. With no remembrance of her doubts, Letty ran to him, throwing her arms around his neck. He grabbed her about the waist and whirled her off the ground in a complete circle as his lips closed over hers. "Oh, Craig," she breathed, completely forgetting her intention to berate him about the change in schedule. His kiss reenergized her, sending shafts of response through her entire being. His effect on her was shattering.

"Hi, pretty lady! Where have you been?"

"Buried in gravel and crab apple trees, not to mention a plethora of New England rock."

He chuckled, that wonderful sound that sent shivery goose bumps up and down her spine. "You look beautiful, even with mud on your nose and juniper bushes in your jeans."

"What?" She looked down at herself. Sure enough, there was a twig of juniper stuck in her side pocket. "How did that get in there?"

He reached down to remove it, brushing his hand over her breast in the process.

"Hey!" she hissed, glancing around nervously, "someone might see you!"

"Naw. Ellen went in, and Joey's way down there." He waved his hand in the direction of the grumbling backhoe.

"Was Ellen out by her pool?"

"Yep. She appeared as soon as I revved up the crane, and she just went in about fifteen minutes ago. She almost wore a bikini."

"What do you mean by 'almost'?"

"There was very, very little of it."

"Uh-huh. I suppose you kept your eyes averted."

"Heck no. It was quite a sight. Joey almost dropped the backhoe into the hole he was digging, and I ran the crane right off the mats."

Letty kept her eyes rigidly focused on the ground in front of her. She would *not* allow herself to feel jealous over a silly matter like a man ogling a beautiful, buxom blonde. She tried to avoid looking at her own small breasts.

His deep rumble sounded again. "Your ears are turning

red. Honey, I'm just teasing. Moving the crane is an all-consuming job that requires my full attention. Besides, I am *not* interested in Ellen Prindle."

She looked up at him, a smile tickling the sides of her mouth. "You bum. You know how rattled you get me."

"The rattling is mutual." With his hand shading his eyes, he looked over toward the Grade-all. "I think Joey is ready to call it a day, and I have to lock up the crane. I'll finish moving it in the morning."

Letty's eyes swiftly shifted in the direction of the back-hoe. "Joey? Where is he? What's he doing?"

"Cool your burner, sweetie. He's still cutting the new reroute around the house. He didn't get near your precious garden sites."

"Oh," she exhaled in relief. "Good. Are you coming to my house?"

"I'm sorry, hon." He ran his fingers through his hair. "I have to go home tonight. Jerry and I have plans to review, and our lawyer is checking over the contract from the Vermonters before we sign it. Everything is moving fast, and I have to be there."

"Oh, phooey!"

"My sentiments exactly."

"Craig, what is all this about Vermont? Tell me the truth. Did this just come up, or are you deliberately shifting things around to keep me out of your hair?"

"Letty, no man in his right mind would put in the night I did last night just to prove some silly point. I have an enormous investment in equipment, and I have to keep it all as gainfully employed as possible. That is, has been, and always will be the bottom line."

She stared at her feet for a moment, then shook her head. "Yes, obviously that would be. I'm sorry." She looked up at him. "I keep putting myself in situations with you that call for an apology. You seem to bring out my irrational side, even though you're the one person in the world with whom I most want to put my best foot forward."

His wonderful smile appeared. "All the sides of you I've seen so far are very appealing." His expression turned more serious. "Don't be afraid of me, Letty." Before she could ask what he meant, he said, "By the way, I had lunch with your father."

"You did? How did that come about?"

"I went to your house to see if I could catch you, but obviously you'd left. However, Caleb was there, dropping off some vegetables from his garden. He asked me to come to his place for a sandwich, so I did. Enjoyed it, too."

"Caleb, is it?"

Craig put his arm around her and started to walk her back up the rise toward the driveway.

"Sounds like you two are getting pretty chummy."

"We hit it off real well. He's quite a guy."

"I agree."

"He wants me to dig him a pond."

"He wants *what?"*

"A pond. You know where his land drops down to a wet area at the rear of his house?"

"Yes."

"Well, he'd rather have a pond than a swamp. Actually it'll be real pretty."

"You'd better watch that contract! He's a sharp lawyer, you know."

"We took care of it with a handshake. The good old-fashioned method."

"I'm glad you had a chance to spend some time with him." She looked at him wistfully. "I hope I get to meet your parents soon."

He stopped suddenly and turned to her. "Letty, why don't you come home with me tonight?"

She stared at him in disbelief. "Tonight!"

"Letty!" His voice had a new urgency. "Why not? I could lock up here while you go home to clean up and throw something into a suitcase, then I could come over and take a shower and call my folks from your house. We could be there for dinner by eight, and at least you'd have a chance to meet them. We could come back here early in the morning."

She hesitated. Actually, she'd been thinking in terms of

being in bed by eight. But the prospect of spending all that time with Craig was tantalizing. "What about your meeting with your brother and lawyer?"

"They could come to my parents' house. We could take care of that while you talk to my folks."

She looked into the deep-sea eyes and drowned. "Okay."

They arrived at his parents' house shortly after eight o'clock. Letty was immediately engulfed in Sullivans. They were all there, smiling, friendly. His parents welcomed her into their midst with Irish enthusiasm and open-hearted acceptance.

She caught them, several times, watching her and Craig with smiles on their faces. They really *want* me to be the right one for him, she thought. She liked all of them—his parents, his brothers, his sisters-in-law.

His mother was plump, cheerful, and efficient. She had whipped up a dinner that would have taken Letty three days to prepare. After dinner Letty carried a load of dishes into the kitchen. "Now you let the others do that, dear," Mrs. Sullivan insisted. "Sit down on that stool and talk to me."

While she filled the dishwasher, Maggie Sullivan pulled most of Letty's life story from her. "I've done all the talking," Letty finally protested, "and I'd planned to pump you for information about Craig."

"Next time I'll tell you all about him from his birth to the present day. I promise. All of it is good, every bit. Of course I may be just slightly prejudiced . . ." The two women laughed. "But Craig is a wonderful man, loving, thoughtful, kind. His one problem is that he works too hard."

Letty burst out laughing and laughed until tears came to her eyes. "I'm sorry," she sputtered, "but that expression is becoming epidemic. My father says the same about me constantly!"

"Then that settles it! The two of you belong together. I knew it the moment you walked in. With that fiery red hair and the sparkle in your eye. I said to myself, 'Now, there's a match for my son!'"

Letty looked at her in open-mouthed astonishment. "Tell

me the truth. Have you already met my father?"

Mrs. Sullivan turned to her with a puzzled frown. "Why no, Letty, but we're certainly looking forward to it. I do hope it'll be soon."

"Well, one thing's certain: You and my dad will get along famously!"

By the time the evening had ended Letty already felt like one of the family. As Craig opened his car door for her he asked, "How did you like them?"

"I think they're wonderful. It's fun being immersed in a large family. It's a new experience for me." Letty's motor was still revved up, her tiredness forgotten. As they turned the corner at the end of the block she asked, "Where do you keep all your equipment?"

"I beg your pardon. It surprises and distresses me to think you consider my equipment missing."

She laughed. It occurred to her that she laughed a lot with Craig. "Your vital equipment is present and accounted for. I meant the auxiliary stuff, like backhoes and bull-dozers."

"Oh, the heavy-duty equipment."

"Well now, I wouldn't call what I've already seen light-weight."

"You're evil."

"I know. And being evil feels so good."

"I think it's time to get home to bed."

"Couldn't you just swing by and show me your office?"

"Now?"

"Uh-huh."

"Trouble. What I have here on my hands is lots of trouble." With a steady underscore of grumbling he made the ten-minute detour. "Going sightseeing at midnight, for crying out loud. Just remember, when we have to stumble out of bed at five A.M., that this was your idea."

"I promise."

Craig pulled up in front of a high chain-link fence and got out to unlock the gate. Then he stepped through and flicked on some outside lights, which illuminated a huge structure with an immense overhead door at one end.

When he climbed back into the car, Letty exclaimed, "Wow! That's impressive!"

"A lot of the machines are out, but I can show you the offices and the shop."

The offices were attractive and neat, and the shop, full of machinery and tools and paraphernalia, was enormous. "My gosh, Craig, I can't believe you've accumulated all this on your own. That's quite an accomplishment."

"It's not all paid for, but almost. Of course, the minute I pay off one machine, I buy another. Although I have practically everything I need now." His face beamed with pride as he gazed around his shop. When his eyes met hers, a touch of doubt invaded them. "Does it bother you that I can't promise you complete financial security?"

She stepped into his arms. "Financial security I don't need. Emotional security is what I need."

He looked down at her, his expression serious. "So do I, Letty. So do I."

By the time they reached his house, Letty was more than ready for bed, but more questions kept popping into her mind. As she entered his front hall she said, "Craig, I notice that your father limps. Why is that?"

Craig went into the living room to turn on some lights, and she followed. "Dad used to be a carpenter, but he fell off a tall ladder when he was about fifty. Shattered a hip. It took quite a while to heal."

"How awful!"

"No, it was the best thing that ever happened to him. He couldn't move around so freely, so he did something he always wanted to do. He bought a hardware store. He loves hardware. Now he has three of them, all going great guns. My brother Allan works with him. Dad's had more fun with his business than most men do with a hobby. He'll probably never retire."

"It sounds like you have a very enterprising family."

"That they are. Dad has always been a risk-taker. I guess that's where I get it. As well as hardware, he loves land. He started buying land with the first money he ever made, and he's been doing it ever since. Luckily, he always liked land that overlooked water, so what he bought is worth a goodly amount today."

"Well! Here I had you pictured as a poor struggling man from a poor struggling family, and now the truth slowly emerges. What we have here is a full-fledged Sullivan empire!"

"Well, a mini-empire maybe. But we're chronic reinvestors, so there's not much opulence to be found, except at Glenn's house. He enjoys living up to the image of the successful doctor."

"Does that bother the rest of you Scrooges?"

"Not at all. We take full advantage. We use his swimming pool and his tennis court and go to his fancy parties. Now, let's go to bed. We have to get up in exactly"—he checked his watch—"four and a half hours."

Their lovemaking was warm and sweet and rather subdued. They were both terribly tired. Letty lay in his arms afterward, content, happy. She moved away just enough to be able to study his handsome profile. She could imagine the number of women who had looked at that face longingly, picturing themselves as Mrs. Craig Sullivan. She snuggled close again, a smile on her face as she fell asleep to dream about being Mrs. Craig Sullivan.

The morning ride back to Massachusetts was done mostly in silence; they were two sleepy people. Craig dropped her at her house to pick up her car, and with a good-bye kiss he headed off to finish moving his crane. Letty intended to pick up some sandwiches and go have lunch with him. By noon the plan had been completely obliterated from her mind.

This morning made the preceding one look like a piece of cake. Everything went wrong at the Fraziers'. The water hose split and had to be replaced. Jim's chain saw flew apart in his hands while he was felling a tree that was in the way, and one of the flying parts grazed his arm. Despite his loud protests, Letty insisted on taking him to the emergency room at the local hospital to have it checked. It was easily treated, but by the time they returned, thirty-four shrubs had been delivered to the site, thirty-one of which were the wrong order and had to be taken back.

It wasn't until three-thirty that afternoon that Letty even thought about the Prindle job. "Yikes!" she said to Jim. "I'd better run over and see what's happening. They must be getting close to the planting areas by now, and Craig was going to start digging the pond."

"How long will that take?"

"I must admit I've never asked. I'd guess it would take several days."

"Did you get a chance to move that little group of Limnanthes we found?"

"Good grief! I didn't! Luckily they're clear over the far side, and I'm sure he hasn't gotten that far. But now I *know* I'd better go! What a loss that would be!" She took off at a brisk trot toward her car.

Limnanthes, or meadow foam, was a lovely, delicate flower that grew wild in wetlands but was usually found in such states as California and Oregon. Letty had been ecstatic when she discovered it, nestled in a sheltering stand of tall grasses that was surrounded by sedges, or "mud ducks," as Craig called them. She wanted to wait until the last moment so she could take them up and replant them in as short a time span as possible.

She made herself slow down as she entered the Prindle driveway. It would be unseemly to come screeching up to a stop in front of the house. As soon as she parked, she jumped out of the car and ran around to the back to get her small, long-bladed shovel and a piece of burlap to wrap the plants in until they could be repositioned. There was the steady drone of large machinery in the air; both the crane and the Grade-all must be at work.

The moment Letty reached the back of the house, she knew she had trouble. The creek was almost to the pond site, and there was a decided departure from the plans. Instead of a lovely, gentle curve around the spot where the English garden was to go, the line of the creek was almost straight, and the slope behind it that was to serve as a background and be planted in tall perennials had been flattened.

With mounting ire, she turned her gaze to the moving crane. Its tall boom was swinging. It stopped, dipped, and scooped up a bucketful of mud, which it dumped on the far edge. There was an enormous pile of black mud in front, waiting to be moved up to another wet area that was to be filled in. Even though the heap almost cut off the area behind, she could see enough to know that the pond was almost completely dug, and that the great bucket was gouging holes in the earth right around where the precious meadow foam was planted.

"Craig!" she shrieked. The movement of the boom continued. Obviously she couldn't be heard over the racket. She glanced around, aware that she had screamed at the top of her lungs. There was no one in sight. Suddenly the reason why the area was vacated became clear as a strong, rancid smell hit her nostrils. It resembled the odor of manure, and it emanated from the digging sites.

With shovel in hand, she took off down the slope, waving her other arm frantically, trying to catch Craig's attention. He must have spotted her, because the crane stopped moving, but he didn't get out. She could see him leaning out the window of the cab, with his hand shading his eyes, looking in her direction.

When she reached the outskirts of the area, her feet began to sink into the rank-smelling muck. "Ooh!" The disgusted exclamation slipped out as the stink assaulted her nose. "Yuck."

Craig climbed out of the crane housing and stood on the top of the track. "Letty!" he yelled. "Get out of there! That's all soft mud. You'll sink!"

"Thanks for the news!" she yelled back. There was a hysterical pitch to her voice. She stood on unsolidly planted feet that sank deeper and deeper into the noxious goo. "What the heck is going on?" She waved frantically toward the too-straight creek bed.

"What?"

"I said . . ." She couldn't yell any louder. "Why don't you come here so I can talk to you?"

"What?" He reached in and turned the motor down some more.

She restrained the temptation to throw the spade at him. "Come here so I can talk to you!" The order was snapped out at top volume.

"Are you nuts! I'm not going to walk across that mud. It stinks!"

"You bet your bippy it stinks, and I'm standing in it!"

"Well, why don't you get yourself out of it?"

"The creek is wrong!"

"I know."

"You *know?* Of all the stupid—then why is it wrong?"

"Joey made a mistake."

"Craig! You're the high and mighty know-it-all who told me his men don't *make* mistakes."

"Cool down, Letitia. You're making one, too."

"Don't you tell me what to do! You can't even do your own job right. I have to go over there." She motioned wildly toward the far side where the wildflowers had been. All she could see was a raft of mud. "Dammit! What have you done with my Limnanthes?"

"What the hell are you talking about?" Craig's usually smooth-knit disposition was visibly snagged.

"My Limnanthes! It was right over there. Do you have any idea how scarce they are around here?" Her voice was a rusty squeak.

"I don't know what the devil you're talking about." Craig's was an ominous rumble.

Letty began the tortuous trek around the newly created mud hole, her feet sinking deeper and deeper with each step. "Where is it? What have you done with it?"

"You were supposed to have everything out of the way by now."

"Why didn't you tell me you'd finish the pond in one day?"

"You didn't ask."

"It probably wouldn't have done me any good to ask."

She laboriously dragged one foot out of the mud and placed it in front of her, then yanked at the other. "You don't seem to be able to make up your mind when you're going to do anything anyway!"

"Letty, you're behaving like a blithering idiot! Will you get yourself out of my way and let me finish this pond?"

"Don't you talk to me as if I were a child!" She tried to stamp her foot but only succeeded in creating a whooshing sound as the foot pulled halfway out of the muck and sank again.

"Letitia Aldridge, get your redheaded temper in hand and your mud-covered ass out of my way!"

She had managed, against all odds, to get to the spot that had held the dainty flower. It was nothing but a muddy hole. "What have you done with it? It was right here!"

Craig was leaning against the housing, his arms folded, a dark glower on his face. "If it was right there, it is now in my bucket, and it will soon be right over there." He pointed emphatically at the tall pile of mud.

"No!" she yowled, mucking her way painfully toward the bucket, which was just out of reach. "Craig, move it over so I can see if it can be saved."

"Letty, for crying out loud, you've gone berserk!"

"Please!" she wailed.

That seemed to be the magic word. He climbed back into the cab, and the motor roared. With incredible precision, he hoisted the massive bucket and set it down right in front of her, then turned down the motor again and stepped back outside. "Now what?"

She trepidatiously picked her way to the bucket and peered in. There, in the giant glob of mud, was one little leaf of her sought-after plant, sticking its tip out of its imprisoning muck. With renewed purpose, she yanked one leg out of the mud and heaved it over the edge of the bucket.

"Letty, what in the name of all that's sane are you doing? Get out of there!"

Without further ado she freed her other leg and hoisted herself into the oversized pail. Ignoring Craig's continuing admonitions, she bent down to poke around the poor little flower. It was clearly beyond reclamation. Kneeling in the malodorous mire, she shook her fist at the alien being on the machine. "You assassin!" she screeched. "You've killed it!"

Her hold on her temper, always tenuous at best, failed completely. She became a virtual hellcat. "Dammit, you incompetent, ill-programmed nincompoop! You've destroyed a genuine Limnanthes Douglasi and screwed up a whole creek bed! You can't do anything right!"

"That does it!" With no further comment, Craig climbed back into the machine, revved up the motor, and started to lift the bucket.

"Ahhhh!" Letty let out a wail of part fury and part fright. "You let me down this minute!" Her furious voice split the air, and even Joey, far across the lawn, shut off his backhoe and stood on the seat to watch.

"Yes, ma'am." She could see the retort, made through clenched teeth, rather than hear it. With growing alarm she realized she had gone too far, and Craig was blowing.

Letty clutched the sides of the bucket, her heart pounding a frantic staccato as she rose higher and higher in the air, swung slowly over the muddy water, and started to descend. In a blinding, appalling flash, his intention became clear to her. "No!" she shrieked, but the bucket just kept lowering. She could see the grim smile on the villain's face as he disregarded her continuing screams. Despite her violently voiced objections, the bucket made its inexorable drop, steadily, in slow motion, dogged. She felt the cold water wet the mud around her feet, then seep up her legs and ripple around her thighs. "Craig! No more!"

She could barely hear him, but the angry tone carried through. "Say *please!*"

It almost choked her, but she pushed it out. "Please!"

"Louder!"

That deplorable beast! She knew what she'd like to say to him! For once she let her predicament call the shots "Please!" she shouted at the top of her register.

The boom rose and the drag line tightened. She watched in awed outrage as the crane swung her container around and lowered her to the ground just beside the pile of mud. The sound of the motor dropped again. "Get out, Letty. I'd like to drop you on your undisciplined can, but you might get hurt."

She clambered over the side, a moving mud pie. When her feet were once more on solid ground, she whirled to face her tormentor. "You jackass! You bastard! You—"

"Shut it off, Letty, or I'll drop your damned flower on your head! It's the only thing not covered with mud so far."

Her head whipped up, and she saw the bucket, full of dripping mud, hovering above, just slightly to her right. With mounting rage she watched Craig climb out of the housing and stand, fists on his hips, glowering at her. She took a few steps away, then spun around as Craig turned to reenter the cab. With one swift gesture, she bent, scooped up a clump of mud, and threw it. She scored a direct hit. It caught him right in the back of the neck, split, and oozed down his collar.

For one frozen instant they both stood still; then Craig jumped into the cab and grabbed the controls, and Letty turned and started to run, her speed hampered by her mud-soaked sneakers. A quick glance over her shoulder showed her that Craig had driven over the muddy section and was jumping down from the machine. He was chasing her! She tried to run faster, but it was like a bad dream. Her soggy feet refused to be rushed.

The bad dream continued. She felt herself grabbed around the waist, lifted, and carried like a sodden rag doll back toward the mud. "You let me go! Damn you to hell, you let me go!"

Without a sound, aside from the stomp, stomp of his boots on the hard lawn, followed by the squish, squish as he reached the soft mud, he carried her to the edge of the pond and, without a moment of hesitation, tossed her in.

The drop was more a splat than a splash, since the water was only about a foot and a half deep at that end, but the damage to her dignity was devastating. She dragged herself out of the water, finding a firmer gravel bottom in the pond than she found when she stepped out of it. "You . . . you . . ."

She could only sputter; no words would form. Besides, she couldn't think of anything foul enough to call him.

"Get out of here, Letty." His tone was flat and hard and ferocious. "Get out of my way so I can finish my job."

"I'll get out of your way! I'll get out of your way and out of your life! Your job isn't all that'll be finished!" She was damned if she'd cry!

"That's just fine with me." He spun around, stamped back to the crane, and climbed up and into the seat. Without even looking her way again, he headed the machine back to where it had been.

Somehow Letty got herself back to her car, minus her shovel and any remnant of her pride. The young man named Joey was standing at the side of the driveway. He approached her, a look of complete bewilderment on his face. "Are you all right, Mrs. Aldridge?"

She tried her voice. A little of it eked out. "Yes."

"Boy. I've never seen Craig that mad. I guess I owe you an apology."

She looked at him, her own face reflecting his bewilderment. "Why?"

"I probably got him started. He was real upset because I read the plan wrong and made a mistake. I was just correcting it."

Somehow Letty knew she didn't want to know, but she asked anyway. "What mistake?"

"I dug the creek straight where it should have curved and flattened the wrong hillock. Mrs. Prindle came out and looked at it before she left and said it was okay with her if you didn't mind, but Craig said 'No way.' He said he'd promised it would be right, and it just plain had to be redone."

"Oh Lord." Letty sank into the driver's seat of her car, taking no heed of the mess she made. "Oh Lord," she muttered again as she drove off.

- *10* -

LETTY STRIPPED IN the garage and threw all her clothes into the trash. She never wanted to see or smell any of them again. It was probably the most senselessly extravagant gesture she'd ever made, but sense had nothing to do with it, any of it.

She found an old pair of boots by the back door and slipped her feet into them. Even stark naked she was a walking mud trail.

It took a full half hour in the shower before she felt clean. There was nothing she could wash with, shampoo with, or swallow that would help the way she felt inside.

When she was finally scrubbed and dried and clothed in clean jeans and a shirt, she plodded downstairs to the kitchen with Pudge close behind. He had trailed her from room to room, his eyes wide and inquisitive, obviously wondering what was wrong with his person.

Letty took a can of cat food from the cupboard, then set it on the counter while she mixed herself a scotch and water. "First things first," she informed the waiting animal. She put his food into a dish and set it on the floor, then, drink in hand, went to the living room to collapse in a big overstuffed easy chair.

Almost immediately Pudge was in her lap, standing to give her three nose-bump kisses before curling up into his purr position. Her hand moved over his silky fur as she sipped her scotch, staring off into space, too deadened inside to process anything. Bad-tempered burnout, her mind suggested.

"You wouldn't have believed me today," she whispered to Pudge, her hand smoothing over and over and over his coat. It was far more comforting to her, she was sure, than to him. "I just plain lost it, Pudge. I threw an all-out, two-year-old's temper tantrum and got the equivalent of a good spanking."

As soon as the words left her mouth she started to cry. She cried and cried and cried, great heaving sobs that came from somewhere below her belt and shattered her all the way up.

Pudge was distraught. He nuzzled her chin and bumped her nose and, with his inquiring *prring?* sound rubbed his cheek against her hand. Poor thing. How could he know how to handle this? She hadn't had a real cry in years. Not since . . . all those years ago . . . the last time she'd really exposed her emotions. Why had she subjected them to devastation a second time?

Letty was so exhausted when the crying jag was over that she locked the doors, put on a flannel nightie—because, despite the warm weather, she was shivering—and crawled into bed.

She lay, still shaken by reverberating aftershocks, clutching her long-haired friend who was loudly purring, more from anxiety, she suspected, then contentment. "Well, Pudge," she mumbled, "I opened the box and let the real Letitia stand up, and she promptly fell flat on her face in the mud." Her body heaved once more and settled. Within minutes she had dropped into deep, obliterating sleep.

* * *

For the next three days she was a working robot. She felt hung over, besieged by all the punishing consequences of a week-long binge. But this binge happened to have been emotional. She stayed as far from the Prindle property as was possible, even driving extra miles to skirt the area. She did not allow thought or feeling. She immersed herself in labor, toiling right along with the men until she was ready to drop, then staggering home to a brisk shower, a scant dinner, and bed.

Fortunately, her father was trying a complicated court case, so he didn't call. She had never been successful at avoiding Caleb's insightful eye, and she needed to stay out of touch with her treacherous emotions. It had been no mistake, all that time, to bottle them up. It had been years since her temper had leaped from a fitful flicker to a fire-spurting volcano.

Craig seemed to incite the raging crazies in all her re-actions, and she couldn't handle it. Her hot-headed child-ishness had earned her just what she deserved, and she was having an awful time preserving her anger at Craig. It was being crowded out by a cold, gripping shame. Craig was undoubtedly congratulating himself for having escaped one more mistake. Maybe she should be congratulating her-self for the same thing.

When she dragged herself into the house at the end of a grueling Saturday the telephone was ringing shrilly. She grabbed it, impatiently slapping down the little hope-creature that reared its head within. "Hello?"

"Letty? It's Duane."

"Oh, Duane!" Hope doesn't live here anymore, she thought. "How are you?"

"Well . . . all right. I miss you."

She sank down on the stool, amazed at how comforting it was to be talking to good old safe, dull Duane. She never went out of control with him. He didn't stir up anything. "I've missed you, too, Duane. I didn't want to hurt you. I hope you believe that."

"I know you'd never hurt anyone intentionally, Letty. You're far too sweet for that."

Sweet? Me? "Why, thank you. That's very kind of you."

"I was wondering . . . is there any reason why we can't see each other occasionally? I won't pressure you to turn it into anything serious again."

No pressure, nothing serious . . . bland. It sounded perfect. "Why, no, Duane, there's no reason we can't see each other." Not anymore.

"In that case, I'll strike while the iron's hot."

Duane had always been a fount of clichés, her mind observed. Shut up, she scolded it.

"How about dinner tonight?" he said eagerly.

She couldn't. She was so tired. Then a picture of the empty, forlorn evening ahead flashed through her mind. At least Duane talked a lot, and he was entertaining. It would fill part of the void. "That sounds fine, Duane. I've been working all day and have to work again tomorrow, so I hope you'll understand if I poop out early."

"Sure." His short, barking laugh sounded. "I'm used to adjusting to your schedule." Music to her ears. "How about if I pick you up at seven? Does that give you enough time?"

She glanced at her watch. It was a little before six. "That'll be fine. I'll see you then."

A consoling sensation of familiarity pervaded her shower and dressing. She was getting ready for a date with Duane. Back to a nice, safe—her mind balked at the word *rut*.

She avoided Pudge's eyes as she fed him. It was only her imagination that he looked disapproving. Undoubtedly Duane was right: Cats were just dumb animals, unable to process thought. She glanced uneasily over her shoulder. Pudge was glaring at her. "Letitia," she lectured herself aloud, "Pudge *cannot* read minds. That's foolishness!" Then why was he retreating to his sulking place under the sofa? She refused to explore it further.

On the way to the restaurant she grasped at the soothing sameness, the touch of serenity, that came from being with Duane. Surely, the gnawing, gnashing turmoil way down inside would disappear. It simply had to. She didn't want feelings of such magnitude. Better to be safe. Better to be in control.

She held tightly to the premise all evening, shutting out an insistent little voice that kept equating "control" with "monotony."

Even though the next day was Sunday, it held no rest for Letty. By the time she drove her weary body home, it was late afternoon. To her dismay, she saw that her father was there. He had let himself in and was sitting on the sun porch with Pudge in his lap. Letty pulled together all available reserves and went in to greet him. "Hi, Dad." Her greeting was accompanied by a weak smile.

"Letty." Caleb stood and turned to her. His face had a sunny, benevolent shine. So he didn't know. "How're you holding up?" He held her by the shoulders and surveyed her. "You look awful."

"Thanks, Dad."

"Letty, I know I'm always after you about your work habits, but this is ridiculous. You look ten pounds thinner. What have you done to yourself?"

It was called suffering, but she had dragged him through that with her once before and she wouldn't do so again. "Now, Dad, you'll never stop regarding me as your little girl. Len is out with a bad back, and it's done awful things to our work load, that's all. We're catching up now. I'll be fine."

"Huh!" Caleb looked unconvinced.

She rushed to change the subject. "How was *your* weekend? Did that case you've been working on keep you busy?"

"Well . . . no. As a matter of fact"—he glanced down at his feet, looking decidedly uncomfortable—"Brenda kept me busy."

"Brenda?"

"You know . . . I mentioned her."

"Brenda?" Letty searched her memory. "Oh, is she the lady you were playing golf with? The one who made your heart go pitter-patter?"

"She's the one."

Now why did Brenda loom as an intruder in her mind? Not too much mystery in that one, she informed herself.

That's Psych I. Right now she felt like a hurt little girl, and she wanted her daddy to herself. Swallowing hard, she asked, "And what did you and Brenda do to pass the time?" Letty, she admonished herself, drop the poor-little-me tone.

Caleb didn't seem to notice. "We had a round of golf and dinner at the club last night. I'm afraid I bored her by cluck-clucking over my daughter and her new beau—you digging in the dirt in Massachusetts and Craig digging in the mud in Vermont. She agreed it seemed a strange way to carry on a courtship." He stopped, studying her quizzically. "Letty, what's wrong?"

And she thought she was doing so well at covering up! She turned toward the kitchen. "How about a drink?"

"Why are you dodging my question?"

Letty stopped, her shoulders as well as her spirits drooping. "Dad, I hate to dampen your spirits, but Craig and I are . . . well, I guess the term would be *kaput*." Her glance flickered across his face and away. She couldn't bear what she saw there.

"What happened?"

"I can't talk about it, Dad. I'm sorry, but I just can't. Not yet."

"All right, that's your prerogative. Do you want some company tonight, or do you need to be alone?"

"Well, to tell the truth, I'm going to a movie with Duane."

He looked as though the words had slapped him across the face. Her stomach muscles clenched.

"Duane. I see. Well then . . . I'll talk to you tomorrow." Visibly gathering himself together, he walked over to bestow a quick kiss on her cheek before heading for the door. "Call if you need me."

"I will . . . both. I'll call, and I'll need you."

Caleb turned and looked at her for a moment, an expression of deep sadness on his face. "See you later, honey."

"Okay, Dad." There was a fierce stinging behind her eyes that she flatly refused to surrender to. As soon as he left she went, with determined gait, up the stairs to get washed up, trying to ignore the voice inside that told her she already was.

* * *

The movie must have been funny. Constant laughter erupted around her, but for some reason the humor eluded her. Duane left her at her door, limiting himself to a friendly peck on the cheek. She had to admit that Duane did not seem to be much of a panacea tonight. Letty was so glad to be home she almost cried. But then, she almost cried over just about anything lately.

When she climbed into bed, she checked the rundown for Monday on the calendar by the phone, wondering where she would ever find the energy to deal with all those obligations. Her eyes scanned the squares that represented her days, each one crowded with inked-in notes. Luckily the planting at the Prindles' was not due to start for two weeks. She prayed she'd be able to walk onto that property without having interior fits by then.

She started to turn out the light, then looked down at the tightly curled white form at the farthest corner of the bed. "Pudge, I know you're mad at me about Duane, but don't desert me now. I need a friend."

There was no movement for about thirty seconds; then Pudge slowly stood, stretched elaborately, and picked his way up the length of the blanket to her side. He put his two front paws on her chest and bumped her nose, then gave two licks to her chin before curling up against her shoulder.

"Thanks, pal." The tears did escape then, running silently down her cheeks. She turned out the light and scooted down under the covers. She fell asleep almost immediately.

There was a ringing sound from far, far away, from some other layer of fuzzy dreamland. Despite her resistance, she could feel herself being torn from the sweet retreat of sleep by the obnoxiously persistent bleat. She fumbled for the light and the phone at the same time. The luminous dial on her clock shone the time. Midnight. Who the devil? "Hello?"

"Letty."

She was instantly awake, alert. "Craig?" It was an uncertain whisper.

"Yes. I know what time it is, and I can't think of any

excuse for calling except that it was late when I headed home from Vermont and I passed my turnoff and just kept coming." It all came out in a rush. "Letty, I need to see you. Can I come over?"

"No!" The hysteria rose just a bit higher than the clamoring need.

"Letty, unlock the door, or be prepared to deal with the police when I break it down and set off your alarm. You think *you* can lose control—wait until you see an aroused Irishman! I'll be there in five minutes!" The phone went dead.

She slumped against her pillow. She *had* seen an aroused Irishman, but she had a feeling he was referring to arousal of a different kind. To hell with him! He was *not* going to order her around! Pudge was sitting up staring at her, his ears laid back in alarm position.

Her intuition told her that, despite Duane's assertions, she'd better heed her cat's signal and unlock the door. Otherwise, well . . . otherwise she would probably be dealing with the local police, a local scandal, and a loco Irishman.

Once she was up she tried to do five things at once: unlock the door, brush her teeth, comb her hair, wash her face, prepare her defenses.

Defenses. The best defense, she reminded herself, is a good offense. Defuse the enemy. She'd hit him where he was vulnerable. She'd use woman's oldest, most reliable weapon to her advantage, and turn him into a quivering glob of Jell-O. With cunning deliberateness she turned on the stair lights and the soft nightlight in her room, pulled off her nightie, mussed her hair—just a little—dabbed some perfume on her wrists, her breasts, and between her thighs, and stood by the window to wait.

While she waited she told herself that this was all in the name of revenge, that her only intent was to get him weakened to a state of satiated languor, then tell him off and throw him out. She also told herself that it was only the anticipation of reprisal that was causing all that excitement inside.

When she heard tires squeal to a stop, a car door slam,

and her front door open, she realized the extent of her self-deception. But it was too late.

Craig stood in the doorway, staring across the room at her naked form, his smoky-blue eyes smoldering beneath the heavy fringe of lashes, the deep cleft in his strong, handsome chin accentuated by the dim light. "Unfair."

"I know."

Then she was in his arms, and nothing else mattered. Nothing in the whole world. It was all still there for them. The caldron that had been simmering on a back burner now boiled over, washing away the days of separation, the anger, the doubt—everything but this wild, untamed hunger.

He swept her up in his powerful arms, carried her the few short steps to her bed, and placed her there, a seething vessel of anticipation, while he pulled off his clothes. Letty watched him take off his shirt and his jeans, shaken by the visual impact of his potent male beauty. Her fingers twitched, frantic to touch the kid-glove-smooth skin. Her lips were dry from eagerness, but every other part of her body felt richly lubricated by the same thing.

Then he was on her, his flesh against hers, flicking on a thousand switches of high-voltage current that jump-started batteries everywhere there was skin on skin.

"Letty!" His guttural exclamation twanged through her, activating a clamorous hubbub of vociferous demand. Every particle of her screamed for him, "Here! Here! Touch me, feel me, take me, devour me!"

Her lips leaped to life beneath his, opening wide to receive sustenance from his mouth, sucking nourishment for the soul from him.

There were a hundred sensual receptors in the palms of her hands, sending delicious messages to her brain. They moved to the sides of his face, coaxing his soft lips to her nipple. When they closed around it, she cried aloud, a bray of acclamation to unbridled abandon.

He kissed her everywhere, his mouth a moving rabble-rouser, inciting riots in her flesh, her acquiescent, readily compliant flesh, which instantly offered itself up to any cause for this reward.

Then her own mouth tingled its demand for equal opportunity. She signaled her desire for him to lie back while her lips and tongue and teeth tasted, nibbled, feasted.

At last he growled "Enough, enough!" and roughly rolled her to her back. He hovered above her for an agonizing moment, his eyes painting her with their blue desire, his breath coming in thick gasps. "Letty!" The velvet voice caressed her. "Letty, I love you so!" He plunged into her, filling to overflowing her cask of vintage happiness. Everything in her welcomed him, opened to him, embraced him.

"Oh Craig!" she exhaled. "I love you, too. Love you, need you, want you." Their bodies moved in familiar concert. Rippling contractions rose within her, sending her soaring to that edge where control didn't exist and bliss exploded into a cacophonous serenade of cymbals, trumpets, bells, and blaring horns—a pandemonium of pleasure.

"Craig!" she cried aloud, no longer shackled by needs of restraint or concerned with control. Control was squandered, tossed away, disposed of. She was freed, unleashed by his reception of her passion, his undisguised hunger for her, his acceptance of all of her. The loosened tiger within romped and cavorted in glee, its claws sheathed, its teeth used only for raucous grinning. Now it crouched, ready, ready, ready . . . then sprang in an exultant leap to the highest branch of the highest tree, roaring its jubilant cry of ecstatic liberation.

"Honey, honey, my lovely Letitia." Craig's silk-soft voice thrummed the special love song of spent rapture. His arms tightened their hold, and his lips joined hers in a kiss of thankful reunion as they lay locked together, loathe to sever the connection.

"Craig"—her voice was a plea—"did you mean it?"

"Mean what?"

"That you love me."

He pulled back just far enough to look into her eyes. "Letty, how could you doubt it? Isn't it more than apparent that I love you?"

She tucked her head back under the shelter of his chin. "I thought . . . after the last time I saw you . . . that you'd never want to see me again."

Of all things, he chuckled, the waves of laughter rumbling through her body. "You did make me pretty darn mad."

"I might say the same for you, mister."

"Uh-huh. We might have to shorten our estimated lifespan together to *two* and a half years."

Letty was very quiet for a few long breaths; then she blurted, "Craig, I should tell you something."

"Okay."

"I've gone out with Duane."

There were a few more longer, silent breaths. "Why?"

"I . . . don't quite know. He called, and it felt so . . . safe."

"Letty, what are you afraid of?"

"Oh, Craig, I wish I really knew. It's just . . . well, it's been such a long time since I *yearned* for someone. And now I yearn for you all the time. And along with that, all of my feelings seem to be whipping up to full gear again."

"I should think you'd be glad to have them all working. Otherwise you miss so much."

"So much what? Pain? Disillusionment? Humiliation?"

"Letty . . ." His fingers touched her lips. He was frowning slightly, looking thoughtful and concerned. "I'm not John Aldridge, honey. I'm far from perfect, but I'm not a bastard. You made a mistake. So did I—and I couldn't even claim youth as an excuse. But you and I together . . . we're right. I know we are!"

"I know, I know. Oh, my love, it's not *you* who scares me. It's the streak of wildness in me. I thought maybe I'd lost it, until you came along."

Craig shifted his weight, repositioning himself on the mattress alongside her but not loosening his hold. "Letty, my darling, you're hot-headed and hot-blooded and marvelous, when you let yourself be. You're also one of the most thoroughly disciplined people I've ever met, when you *need* to be. You can be a little wild with me; it doesn't frighten me."

"But it frightens me. We seem to have so many conflicts—our stubbornness, our need to govern our own lives—

I'm not sure we could work them out."

Craig hoisted himself up on one elbow and looked down at her, running loving fingers over her cheek. "Honey, what problems do we have that are all that awesome? We're two strong-minded people who have lived alone long enough to get set in our ways. So we have a little squabble now and then. Is that going to kill us?"

Yes, yes, it might! How could she explain the dreadful swell of fear inside when she didn't understand it herself? "You always seem so sure of yourself, so strong. Aren't you ever just the tiniest bit afraid I'll turn out to be another Evelyn?"

"No. Not even the tiniest bit. There is no resemblance whatsoever." He chuckled. "Well, maybe just a shred showed up when you started to remodel my yard."

"Did she try to remodel your yard?"

"No, my kitchen. Remember I told you it took most of a year to get the work done?"

"Yes."

"Well, Evelyn had started to turn it into a white Formica-and-chrome wonder. The real wonder is that I was standing by letting her do it. See? Even strong, sure me can turn into a ninny. Fortunately, she split before it went too far."

"So that's why you snapped at me about not changing things until I moved in!"

"Gut reaction, that's all. I told you I had a few dark corners. Actually, I'll have the whole yard dug up if you like, so you can start from scratch and do as you please. Would that help anything?"

She tried to laugh, but her humor seemed stuck under something heavy. "Don't you have any of that anger left? The anger I spotted the first night you mentioned her?"

"Maybe, but you've been very healing. I'm just so damn grateful I was single and unattached when I met you."

"Craig, I . . ."

"Honey, I honestly don't think we have any massive conflicts. What we do have are some significant scars from our past-imperfect love affairs. Yours consumed a long stretch of your life. Naturally the damage would be worse for you.

I was lucky; Evelyn only botched up a year." He kissed her tenderly. "Let him go, Letty. Get rid of John. It doesn't make a lot of sense, you know, trying to protect yourself from new hurt by hanging on to old hurt."

"Don't be silly...I..." To her astonishment and chagrin, great swells of anguish rolled up, up, and over. She started to cry. For the second time in a week, Letty felt her body totally wrenched by sobs. They shook through her, rocking her with their intensity, until she felt like the victim of a terrible internal earthquake.

Craig held her, fiercely, protectively, murmuring to her, assuring her. "Let it out, honey. Get rid of it. You don't have room for it anymore."

When the storm finally subsided, Craig asked, "Have you ever let yourself cry it out before?"

She shook her head. "This happened the night we had the fight over the pond. But I thought I was just mad."

He tipped her chin up to kiss her swollen eyes, then grinned at her. "I suspect you *were* mad, but at least it was a good, healthy mad with plenty of cause. And how are you feeling now? Still upset?"

She shook her head and sniffed, then wound her arms around his neck and hugged him. "Grateful, oh so grateful to have found you. Oh, Craig, I do love you."

"And I love you. The only thing we'll have to guard against is strangling each other with emotional security."

She actually giggled. "Are you sure you're ready to risk living with me?"

"Well, I knew you were dangerous right from the first. I think I can keep you from turning lethal."

"Oh, you do, huh? You may be surprised."

"It should be quite a learning experience. We can test an old conundrum."

"What old conundrum?" She moved her head over on the pillow.

"What happens when an irresistible force meets an immovable object."

"Oh dear. We may never settle that one."

"Let's hope not." Just as her eyes closed, she heard "Damn!"

Her eyes popped open. "Damn? Craig? What's the matter."

"Ah, honey, I came down here on an impulse. Obviously a first-rate impulse, but, nevertheless, I should head right back. We're still working on that job in Vermont, and it's a bitch. I'm supposed to be there first thing in the morning. If I fall asleep, I'm finished."

"Oh." She caught her pleading words before they could get out. She wanted so much to ask him to stay, but she knew how unfair that would be. He wouldn't be leaving if it weren't necessary. "I agree," she grumbled. "Damn."

As she steeled herself to letting him go, she heard him say, "What's this? We seem to have become a cozy little threesome." She looked up. Pudge had wedged himself between them and was lying, his head next to Craig's, purring. "Pudge . . ." Craig's voice was softly entreating. "Come on. Give me a break. Move over. I have to get up."

"Meow?" Pudge stood, stepped off the pillow and up onto Craig's chest. He stretched his neck forward to give Craig several loving nose-bumps, then settled on his chest, filling the air with his resonating purr.

"Now just how," Craig groaned, "am I to fight all this? It was next to impossible to imagine tearing myself away from your warm, delectable body and your warm, soft bed. Now add to that a warm, purring cat on my chest. Unfair." He stroked Pudge a few times before his hand dropped to his side. "Maybe I'll just rest my eyes for a minute." Within seconds he was sound asleep.

Letty, curled close beside him, glanced up at Pudge. "Thanks, pal," she murmured.

Pudge yawned and, she would have sworn, winked, before settling his head under Craig's chin. Craig and Letty were both very late for work on Monday.

- *11* -

I⊤ WAS EARLY evening on a glorious, nicely hot September first. Letty flew around the house, gathering up what she needed: a towel, two champagne glasses, her worn sneakers. She had quit work at noon and spent some time on personal matters. After all, she had to break the habit of filling every weekend with work. It *was* Saturday, and some people *did* take Saturdays off. She grinned. She'd have to remind her intended of that fact.

Her *intended*. What a pleasant, old-timey word. It fit nicely into her bright, sun-filled, new-timey world.

"Hey, Letty! Are you ready?"

"Yep, be right there." She grabbed her canvas bag and her shoes and headed for the front door. She put them both down when she got there so she'd have her arms free to throw around the neck of her intended and give him a great big kiss. "Gosh, you're sexy," she crooned. "They should build a wire fence around you with a sign that says DANGER, HIGH VOLTAGE."

Craig grinned his sexy grin at her. "That's okay with me, as long as you're inside the fence."

"Okay, let's go. The pond awaits us!"

In high spirits they drove to the Prindles' house. The gate had been opened by the caretaker, since the Prindles were spending the end of August and the beginning of September at Cape Cod. They parked the car and took the supplies out of the back. Craig had brought his inflatable rubber boat and paddles from home, and they eased it out of the wagon, put the canvas bag full of bottles and jars and vials in the middle—along with the bottle of champagne and the glasses—and, each on an end, carried it around the house to the pond.

When they arrived at the water's edge they pushed the bag and bottle to the center of the boat, each grabbed an oar, and gingerly climbed in. The boat sank to the shallow bottom.

"Just a minute." Craig crawled out, pulled off his sneakers and tossed them to the grass, then waded out, pushing the boat deep enough to float. He then scrambled back in, causing Letty to hold her breath until the boat righted itself.

"Okay, time to christen the pond!" Craig picked up the bottle of champagne and, with a loud pop, uncorked it. While Letty held the glasses, he filled them in preparation for toasting the new "wildlife and amenity sanctuary."

As he poured the bubbly liquid, Letty gazed around. The water had cleared to a deep blue, and the mud, which had been graded and seeded, had lost its odor and gained some solidity, as well as the start of a grass cover. The creek, now in the proper contour, held a slight trickle of water, which would increase in the rainy season. The initial plantings had been made in both gardens, but they wouldn't be finished for a few weeks. The place was going to look marvelous.

Letty smiled as she surveyed the area behind the pond. There was a gentle slope set back from the water's edge— the perfect backdrop. Craig had consulted with Dr. Fish, and they had decided there was no danger involved in a slight rise. Not what she had asked for, but almost. Craig had sculpted it in those days after the fight at the pond. She shook her head in wonder. Craig had never doubted that they would get back together.

"You know something, honey?" she murmured.

He found a place in the bottom of the boat for the bottle. "No, what?"

"I think what we've created here is spectacular. In fact, almost . . . monumental."

The laugh lines at the edges of his eyes deepened. "Careful, you might get dunked."

"If I go, you go."

"Of course. Whither thou goest . . ."

"You don't have to promise that for a whole month."

"I promise it right now."

She gazed at him, so full of joy she could have bubbled over without the champagne. "Me, too."

Craig raised his glass and said, "Here's to the pond. This lovely oasis in the midst of all this stark opulence that brought us together!" They clinked glasses and toasted each other. "Now," Craig declared, "for the second stage of our assignment! You hold the glasses, and I'll row us out to the middle."

Once they were there, they took turns, alternately holding the glasses and opening the little containers that had been shipped from a biological supply company in North Carolina. The vials were of different sizes, none large, all full of water and, in most cases, practically invisible organic creatures and greenery. Craig opened the first one, tipped it over the side, and said, "Good luck to you, goniums!" They took time for another toast.

Letty dispersed four jars of copepods and some nitella and let Craig take care of the ostracods and the volvox. The chara took a while because there was so much of it, and they gave an extra toast to the eudorinas and the rotifers. When they were done, they rowed back to shore, laughing and wishing the organisms well.

Craig finished packing up the boat, then raised his glass.

"Here's to you, plankton and squigglies alike. May you multiply, divide, and fill the pond!"

"Hear, hear!" Letty chimed.

She then turned toward the empty house and said, "And here's to Ellen, a really good loser!" She had teased Craig about Ellen's unsuccessful designs on him. But Ellen had come through like a trouper, insisting on giving a combination pool- and garden-warming and contratulations-to-the-new-couple party in their honor. They clinked their glasses and drank a last toast before picking up the boat and heading back to the car.

They were going to Caleb's house for dinner.

The friendship between Caleb and Craig had grown steadily. Letty was convinced that if she broke up with Craig at this point, her dad would never forgive her.

They had to swing back by Letty's place to pick up a surprise for her father. When they reached his house, they settled the surprise in a corner of the garage, then stored the boat at the side. The christening rite was to be repeated here as soon as there was enough water in this pond to float a boat. Unfortunately, there were not four natural springs here, and this was the low-water time of year.

Caleb had cooked a leg of spring lamb and churned up some homemade raspberry ice cream. Pudge, who had been invited, too, and picked up earlier by his host, was sound asleep in an easy chair, full of enough tasty tidbits, Letty had no doubt, to fill two cat stomachs.

It was a delightful meal, full of good-humored ribbing and very good food. They all fit together, happy pieces in a jigsaw-puzzle of contentment.

After dinner, Letty sat squeezed next to Pudge in the big chair next to the window and watched the men standing in front of her gesturing and arguing. The pond had grown from the nucleus of an idea to a rather large, almost dry hole.

"What do you think, Craig? Will I have more water next year, or will it still be this dry?"

"Caleb, as I told you when I dug it, it will always be

dry for part of the year unless you put a liner in it."

"Like you'd use in a swimming pool?"

"Same idea. It's an eight-millimeter-thick sheet of vinyl. Very sturdy. It would hold the water all summer."

"Sounds phony. I'm not sure I like it."

"The ducks will never know."

"Are you willing to guarantee that?"

"Yep. First duck complaint, you get a refund."

"You've got yourself a deal." The men shook hands heartily.

Craig looked at Letty. "I hate to say this, but I have to start back soon. We're moving the crane about sixty miles tomorrow, and it means an early start."

"Huh!" she retorted. "My main rival in life has a sixty-foot boom. How do I compete with that?"

Caleb looked from one to the other. "Somehow I doubt that'll be a problem."

"Letty?" Craig touched her arm.

"Oh! That's right!"

On her way out to the garage she heard Craig say, "We have a little gift for you, Caleb..."

Letty went over to the big cardboard box in the corner of the garage and bent down to pick up the tiny, brown-and-buff-colored ball of fluff. It was a chocolate-point Himalayan kitten, a baby girl-cat, so sweet that Letty had had trouble with the prospect of giving her up.

She and Craig had been concerned that her dad would be lonely when Letty married and moved to New Hampshire, particularly since Pudge was to go with them. They had searched far and wide for this kitten, finally locating her in Connecticut.

When she reentered the living room, her father was standing by the window with his back to her, still talking to Craig.

"Dad?"

He turned, his eyes not immediately registering what she held. Then he focused on the wee parcel. Letty put the kitten on the floor. It stretched in true Pudge fashion, looked around, then walked straight to Caleb, sat on his foot, and started to purr.

Pudge looked up from his nap, joining in the silent vigil. Caleb stared down at the small creature on his foot, then bent to pick it up. It was amazing how loudly such a tiny kitten could purr.

"Well, well." Caleb cleared his throat. "What have we here?" He stroked the little head, looking back at the steady blue gaze. His eyes rose to meet Letty's. "Is this my surprise?"

"Yes." She felt a bit weepy. Craig put his arm around her and cleared his throat. They were all a bit weepy.

"Look at us," her dad humbugged, "getting silly over this foolish animal." The foolish animal reached up and licked his chin. Caleb frowned at it. "Been taking lessons from Pudge, haven't you?" He smiled at Craig and Letty. "Thank you. Thank you both." His eyes shifted to Pudge. "And you."

Letty laid her hand on his arm and grinned at him. "I do hope Brenda isn't allergic to cats."

"Brenda loves cats. She'll go nuts over this one."

With Pudge in his box, they all walked out to the car, the new kitten cradled in the crook of Caleb's arm. "Dad, I'm glad you have a girlfriend." She laughed. "I never thought I'd be able to say that!"

"Girlfriend, humph. You make me sound like some silly teenager! And don't start fretting over me, Letitia. After all, I'm not losing a daughter, I'm gaining a son and his whole crazy Irish family." Caleb had gone to New Hampshire with them to a cookout, and Letty had been right. They all took to one another at once.

Craig laughed. "Pretty good deal, eh, Caleb? One of those made-in-heaven romances."

"Well, I am encouraged. You two have been downright docile lately. I thought there'd be at least one more clash by now, what with Letty's temper and your stubbornness."

"Why, Dad," Letty chirped, "we're like two quiet lambs together! We haven't even raised our voices at each other for weeks. I think for once your prognosis is wrong. I just can't imagine Craig and me getting into any more arguments."

Caleb looked at the porch light glinting off Letty's red hair. "Uh-oh," he muttered.

Craig winked at him and said, "Don't worry about it. I'm becoming downright malleable."

"Uh-oh," Caleb repeated.

Letty waved a cheery good-bye to man and kitten as she walked to the car with her future husband.

WONDERFUL ROMANCE NEWS:

Do you know about the exciting SECOND CHANCE AT LOVE/TO HAVE AND TO HOLD newsletter? Are you on our *free* mailing list? If reading all about your favorite authors, getting sneak previews of their latest releases, and being filled in on all the latest happenings and events in the romance world sounds good to you, then you'll love our SECOND CHANCE AT LOVE and TO HAVE AND TO HOLD Romance News.

If you'd like to be added to our mailing list, just fill out the coupon below and send it in...and we'll send you your *free* newsletter every three months — hot off the press.

☐ *Yes, I would like to receive your free SECOND CHANCE AT LOVE/TO HAVE AND TO HOLD newsletter.*

Name _____

Address _____

City _____ **State/Zip** _____

Please return this coupon to:

Berkley Publishing
200 Madison Avenue, New York, New York 10016
Att: Irene Majuk

HERE'S WHAT READERS ARE SAYING ABOUT

Second Chance at Love®

"I think your books are great. I love to read them, as does my family."
   —P. C., Milford, MA*

"Your books are some of the best romances I've read."
   —M. B., Zeeland, MI*

"SECOND CHANCE AT LOVE is my favorite line of romance novels."
   —L. B., Springfield, VA*

"I think SECOND CHANCE AT LOVE books are terrific. I married my 'Second Chance' over 15 years ago. I truly believe love is lovelier the second time around!"
   —P. P., Houston, TX*

"I enjoy your books tremendously."
   —I. S., Bayonne, NJ*

"I love your books and read them all the time. Keep them coming—they're just great."
   —G. L., Brookfield, CT*

"SECOND CHANCE AT LOVE books are definitely the best.!"
   —D. P., Wabash, IN*

*Name and address available upon request

Second Chance at Love®

All of the above titles are $1.95
Prices may be slightly higher in Canada.